W9-BZY-804

## "THERE IS BLOOD IN THE WATER," THE STICKSMAN INTONED.

"Yes, well, you put it there," Aspen said.

"And as I hold the steering pole," the Sticksman said, "so it holds me."

"What does *that* mean?" Aspen managed to croak.

"It means he can't fight," Snail said.

Over the roaring water, Aspen heard a new sound. An eerie hooting, long and low, like the bottom note on one of Moon's bone flutes.

"Fight what?" He finally had breath again.

"Them," the Sticksman said.

The hooting stopped, and the arrows as well, and in the relative silence, Aspen suddenly heard the shouts from shore turn to shrieks of surprise.

And pain.

"The mer," the Sticksman added, a bit too eagerly.

# OTHER BOOKS YOU MAY ENJOY

# ❧ THE ❧
# HOSTAGE
# PRINCE

### THE SEELIE WARS: BOOK I

## Jane Yolen & Adam Stemple

PUFFIN BOOKS
An Imprint of Penguin Group (USA)

PUFFIN BOOKS
Published by the Penguin Group
Penguin Group (USA) LLC
375 Hudson Street
New York, New York 10014

USA * Canada * UK * Ireland * Australia
New Zealand * India * South Africa * China

penguin.com
A Penguin Random House Company

First published in the United States of America by Viking,
an imprint of Penguin Young Readers Group, 2013
Published by Puffin Books, an imprint of Penguin Young Readers Group, 2014

Copyright © 2013 by Jane Yolen and Adam Stemple
Original map conceived by John Sjogren, rendered by Eileen Savage

Penguin supports copyright. Copyright fuels creativity, encourages
diverse voices, promotes free speech, and creates a vibrant culture.
Thank you for buying an authorized edition of this book and for complying
with copyright laws by not reproducing, scanning, or distributing any
part of it in any form without permission. You are supporting writers
and allowing Penguin to continue to publish books for every reader.

THE LIBRARY OF CONGRESS HAS CATALOGED THE VIKING EDITION AS FOLLOWS:
Yolen, Jane, author.
The hostage prince / Jane Yolen and Adam Stemple.
p. cm.—(The Seelie Wars ; book 1)
Summary: "Snail, a midwife's apprentice in the Unseelie Court, meets Prince Aspen, a
Seelie prince being held as a hostage in order to prevent a war. In thinking that they are
stopping the war, they instead trigger one"—Provided by publisher.
ISBN 978-0-670-01434-7 (hardcover)
[1. Fantasy. 2. Princes—Fiction. 3. War—Fiction.] I. Stemple, Adam, author. II. Title.
PZ7.Y78Ht 2013
[Fic]—dc23
2013013478

Puffin Books ISBN 978-0-14-242234-2

Printed in the United States of America

1 3 5 7 9 10 8 6 4 2

For Terri Windling, Ellen Kushner, and Delia Sherman, that magical trio, and Sharyn November, who asked for it—J.Y.

For my favorite changeling, Alison—A.S.

FYDIR

EAL

OLLM

AESTARI PALACE

Graveyard

Black Lake

Here Be Moat Dragons

Seelie Lands

The **SHIFTING LANDS**
*include the following:*

The Speaking Plains

Birch Braes

The Wild Woods

Ea's Falls

The Crooked Steppes

Esker Hills

The Hunting Grounds

Lake Country

# CONTENTS

# HOSTAGE PRINCE
## THE
## PRINCE

# SNAIL WAKES

"Shift yourself, Snail. It's half morning and the queen's baby will be born this day." The midwife gave her apprentice a sharp slap on the rump with the measuring stick, hard enough to sting through the covers. Then she waddled back into the parlor room they shared with the other midwives.

"Mmmmmmf," Snail replied. There'd been a celebration last night with the backstairs folk—the cook boys and ostlers, the dog boys and castle maids—all of them wild with anticipation. Since the queen gave birth only once every hundred years, none of them had ever seen a baby royal. They'd stayed up much too late eating enough cake to feed the entire Unseelie army.

"But why?" Snail had asked the midwife in the first days of her actual apprenticeship. She'd been four at the time, and trying to tie her shoes.

Hands on ample hips, Mistress Softhands replied, "Since the queen lives so long, the palace would be crammed full of royal babes all fighting for a chance at the throne if she had them once a year like ordinary Unseelie folk. And we can't have that."

"But why?" Snail had repeated. Sometimes she was slow at grasping such things. Slow at spells, too. Like the lace tying. She knew she should have mastered that spell by three years old. All the other new apprentices had. And there she was still struggling with it a year past. Usually the laces she'd just bespelled would simply sigh open. Or she'd trip over them minutes after she'd just bound them up. Then Mistress Softhands would scold her. Gently, but firmly. Hold her hands over the laces just so. Correct her spelling.

"But why?"

"Think, Snail, think. It would make all our lives miserable, that would, with dozens of young royals crowding the palace. Spats, quarrels, spells thrown hithery-thithery, duels, wars."

*It makes sense, in a way*, Snail had thought at the time, though later, when she was old enough to know a thing or three about the court, she'd thought differently. There were already spats, quarrels, tongue-lashings, and duels between the royals. And when spells were hurled about carelessly, well, it was the underlings, apprentices, and other non-toffs who bore the brunt of them.

*Wars, though . . . those are few and far between. Too dangerous. And, for the long-lived fey, too final. But at least*, Snail thought, *I'm smart enough not to say so aloud.*

All throughout the royal palace there were spies, turncoats, tittle-tattlers, lickspittles, liars, moles, patrols, lackeys, flunkies, toadies, snoops, spooks, and just plain liars-for-a-penny. An apprentice—even a midwife's apprentice—could just . . . just disappear after having voiced such thoughts to the wrong fey. And no one actually knew who the wrong fey might be until it was too late.

*Best to be leery and wary, than teary and buried,* was the apprentice creed.

"Snail!" Mistress Softhands' voice split the fusty air.

Snail tore off her bedsocks and pulled on fresh underclothes and, after them, her striped leggings. Then she bent over to put on her shoes, good sturdy cowhide shoes with fat, tough laces. Apprentice shoes, not the soft, fawn-skin dancing slippers that the court ladies favored, of course. Or even the calf-leather sandals of the ladies-in-waiting. The stone floors of the palace were far too cold to go around even for a few minutes without some kind of foot cover—unless of course one was a satyr with hooves, or a hall hound with furred feet, or a drow with those clacketing, scaly claws. Any skin-footed fey knew that without shoes on one's feet would turn into ice for the rest of the morning.

Snail held her hands over the laces just so. Said the spell.

> Tie and bind
> Lace to leather,

Keep these pieces
All together.
Ally-bally bargo.

It was a children's spell, of course, but at least one she could count on for as long as needed. And she'd never say it in front of another fey or they'd tease her till she wept. Feys were not supposed to weep unless it was for the death of a queen. Or king.

As she worked the spell, Snail thought to herself, *But really, the queen gives birth only once in a hundred years?* It still made little sense. Snail herself had grown up without any brothers or sisters, and she thought it hard that a royal baby should have to live so lonely a life. Of course a royal baby would have nurses and maids and ladies- or gentlemen- in-waiting, would have cooks, nannies, tutors, and . . .

"And me," she whispered, though she knew that even should she be called upon to help Mistress Softhands with the birth, she'd never be allowed to actually hold the royal baby.

*Or even,* she supposed, *see it again except from very far away.* A midwife's apprentice was hardly a suitable companion for a prince. Or a princess, if the luck ran that way.

*Of course the queen of Faerie,* Snail thought, *hardly needs a midwife. Her babies slip out with a bit of magic and a good dose of warm oil. Or so any outsider might think.*

But royal or not, there were still dangers. No one in the Unseelie Court was likely to forget the baby prince named

Disaster of two hundred years past who'd been hanged in his own cord before a spell could get him out. Since that time, royal births were always attended not only by one or two midwives, but by all of the birthgravers in the kingdom, along with their apprentices. What Mistress Softhands called "pulling up the drawbridge after the moat dragon has wandered in and fouled the Great Hall."

"And wouldn't that have been a sight!" Snail mused, knowing that she wouldn't have been the one to have to clean *that* mess up. That job belonged to the moat boys and the dragon wranglers.

But thinking about it—the fat old moat dragon humping out of the water, dripping pond scum and duckweed, shedding frogs and lily pads, lumping through the portcullis and into the courtyard, scattering the warhorses, making its loopy way into the Great Hall . . . she began to giggle.

"Snail!"

"Moving," Snail answered as she quickly scootched around her bed, throwing off nightgown and nightcap. Fey ears were sensitive to the cold, and even though hers were rounder and shorter than most, and closer to her head, she wore a cap to bed at night. Everyone did.

"Snail!" This time there was steel in Mistress Softhands' voice. She always called three times. *Not the magical three,* she always warned, *but the practical three. Because it takes you three times to do what I ask.*

Snail didn't wait for a fourth call, for if it came, it would be accompanied by a switch and a spell. Usually a turn-into-a-snail spell. Not a real snail, of course. True transformations were royal magic and no one below that status could do them. But it would be an illusion that felt real enough to Snail. For a minute or more she'd look and feel like a single-footed slime creature, the size of the snail relating to how angry her mistress was at the time. Once—it was a truly awful once—she'd been turned into a dog-sized snail for an entire afternoon. Or at least she remembered it that way. Then she was set out on the lip of the castle's well where everyone laughed at her and two of the young dukes threatened to push her in. They were only kept back from accomplishing their threat by Mistress Softhands's secondary ward spell.

Snail knew her name was a joke, given to her when she was three years old. Before that, she had been called "Baby" and then "Child" and sometimes "Little Nuisance" and "Why Did I Bother?" And when Mistress Softhands was really angry with her, simply "You!"

Only "Snail" had stuck.

But at the moment names didn't much matter to her. Her belly hurt from all that cake, and her rump stung from Mistress Softhands' measuring stick, and somewhere during the night's festivities she must have banged the back of her arm, because she could just make out a bruise blossoming there, the color of thistle.

Mistress Softhands stomped into the bedchamber, jowls

aquiver, grey hair threatening to come down from her tightly wound bun, and then wouldn't there be trouble!

Leaping off the bed, Snail cried out, "I'm up, Mistress! I'm up!"

"But not dressed."

Mistress Softhands handed her the striped apprentice dress and white starched apron that she'd taken from the floor. She held it between her thumb and forefinger as if the thing was something stinking, something hauled out of the midden pile.

Snail accepted the dress and apron, her mouth turned down in what she hoped was a penitent's pout.

"Not your dress on the floor again, Snail. Not *today* of all days." Mistress Softhands was aroar and her face practically a wound. "What if the new princeling picks up something ghastly from this garment—a fleshbug or a nose nibbler or . . ."

Head down, her cheeks practically blistering with shame, Snail put the dress on, buttoned it up the front, then tied the apron with a knot in the back, only thinking the tying spell but not daring to say it aloud.

Mistress Softhands held her right palm toward the dress, and Snail flinched. She hated being poked in the stomach and Mistress Softhands knew it. But the midwife had no such intentions. Fingers tight together, she moved her hand in circles.

Absterge, clarify,
Launder, wash, rinse, then dry,
Dredge, dust, depurate,
Scour, scrunge, and expurgate.
All out!

On the last, with a controlled shout, she pushed her hand forward, almost—but not really—touching the dress.

*Now that*, Snail thought, *is a proper grown-up spell.* She couldn't remember half the words and didn't know what the other half meant. Except for wash and rinse. *Oh, and dry!* But now, at least, her dress was clean.

Mission accomplished, Mistress Softhands smiled, smoothed down her own starched white apron, and left the room.

## ASPEN ENTERS THE HALL

*P*rince Aspen stood in his braies and stared into the broad chest at the foot of his bed. Tapping a finger against his cheek, he considered the neatly folded piles of cloth inside.

*Linen hose today,* he thought, *since it is to be a celebration feast.* He reached inside for a pair of periwinkle hose and pulled them on. Tying them at the top, he thought, *And a linen shirt to match.* He rummaged through till he found a fine linen shirt with periwinkle threading. Once he'd hefted it over his head, the shirt hung nearly to his ankles.

"Tunic," he said aloud.

He looked at the bed, where a tunic had been laid out for him. It was a dark, drab green.

"That will never do, Lisbet," he said to the empty room. "It doesn't match the shirt at all. I'll need something brighter. Perhaps in a color more . . . unexpected." He looked in the chest and smiled. "Yes. Red."

Sometimes in the morning, Aspen liked to pretend he was still back home and Lisbet, his old nanny, was helping him choose clothes for the day. Alone in his room, he could pretend the bustle he heard in the halls was made by brownies, not bogles or goblins, and that when he walked out the door, they would all bow to him with bright courtesy and respect and say, "Good morrow, Prince Aspen."

*Actually,* he thought, *the bogles and goblins all bow and say good morrow, too.* He frowned. *But they do it grudgingly.*

Yes, he was a prince here, just like at home. But here he was also a hostage, a prisoner, a bargaining chit to keep the peace. And though the bogles and goblins bowed and scraped as they were supposed to, Aspen knew that if it came to war, their long knives would be in his belly before he could say back to them, "And good morrow to you."

He tried to shake off that dark thought by picturing old Lisbet, but realized he couldn't remember what she actually looked like. It had been seven years since he'd last seen her, before he was sent to the Unseelie king as hostage, in exchange for one of their own. He'd been but a child then.

"And I'm still a child if I think games and imaginings will help me here." Sighing heavily, Aspen closed the chest with a thud and picked up the green tunic.

"Drab dress for another drab day," he said, and yanked the garment over his head. Then, without fixing his hair—a deeper gold than that of the princes of the Unseelie Court—he opened the door and stalked into the hall. He almost tumbled over a small bogle who was on his knees scrubbing the flagstones.

"Good morrow, Prince Aspen," the creature said, somehow managing to bow even lower than he already was while still sending out waves of resentment and disdain. Aspen wanted to kick the ugly little thing. It was a sworn enemy of his people, after all.

But kicking a servant was how an *Unseelie* prince would behave. *And I am Seelie*, he reminded himself. It did no good. He had been at this court too long. Almost half his life.

"And good morrow to you, kind bogle," he said quickly, with a shallow nod of his head, as if giving the creature back its own disdain doubled. Then he trudged down the hall toward the feast hall.

The festivities were already in full force when Aspen arrived.

The Unseelie hardly waited for a civilized hour to start carousing, as Aspen's family would have. There was no decorum to the procedure, no stately procession of courses, no palate cleansers between. The Unseelie sat at their tables—or in some cases, *on* them—and celebrated rude toasts by crashing their tankards together so hard there was as much mead on the floor as in their bellies. They banged spear hafts against the table when they got angry or happy or somewhere in between, and occasionally spitted an unwary hob with the other end. It was a mob scene, unruly and loud. Almost every dinner was like this, and celebrations such as the one they were gathered for—because the queen was due to have a child at any moment—were especially loud. And dangerous. He would have to watch both his back and his stomach.

He admired the serving girls, who managed to scamper from kitchen to table and back again all the while keeping their balance and, at the same time, dodging the various pinches, slaps, and lecherous comments sent their way. It seemed almost as if they had trained with a traveling show of jugglers and jesters, mountebanks, and escape artists.

That thought was so absurd, he laughed at his own imagining.

But the banging and bragging and bashing of spear hafts had reached such a fever pitch already, he had no interest in trying to make his way through the crowd to the king's table where he, as a noble, was expected to sit. Instead he stuck to the wall, and went the slow way around, hoping to avoid notice for as long as possible.

*Though, being the Hostage Prince*, he thought, *means I can never avoid notice for long.*

# SNAIL IN THE KITCHEN

*A*s soon as she was alone again, Snail went over to the mirror and ran her fingers through her cockscomb hair, which was a dull orange and ugly, not a color often seen in the Unseelie lands. She let out a deep sigh. Only she of all the apprentices in the castle seemed to be affected by too much faerie cake, that golden berry cake soaked with a spell made on Midsummer's Eve. Only she ever suffered any consequence from eating it.

"You!" she said, pointing her finger at the mirror. The mirror did not answer her of course. It was not a magic mirror like the queen had, but rather one of the silvered glass shards stolen from some house in the mundane human world.

"Yes?" she answered herself. *If one doesn't have a lot of* close *friends*, she'd often thought, *make a close friend of oneself.* She wasn't sure if she'd made that up or heard it somewhere. Either way, it suited her. Certainly, she knew a lot of apprentices—pot boys and dog boys, kitchen maids and dairy maids, first-year blacksmiths and second-year needle-workers, and a couple of girls learning to be hedge witches, and the like. She danced and sang with them, and they held parties in the servants' hall. But she wasn't sure she'd call any one of them a *close* friend. Just fey folks she knew.

Surely a close friend was something else. Something . . . deeper. Or stronger. *Or—well—closer.*

She shook her head and the mirror girl shook her head back.

"Get going," she admonished her reflection, one finger raised. "You know, the queen is about to . . ."

The angular girl in the mirror with the one green and one blue eye, the hair that no brush could tame for long, the nose too broad for beauty, and the ears too short to hear grass sway, had raised an answering finger.

"I know," she told herself. "I know."

Then she washed in the basin that Mistress Softhands had filled with hot water, though by now it was only lukewarm.

"Blessed be," Snail whispered. Sometimes the midwife was a loving creature. Other times . . . well, Snail didn't like to think about the other times.

First she washed her face, for the new mother would need to look at rosy cheeks. Next, she looped the sleeves of her dress above her elbows, then scrubbed her hands all the way up to where the cloth of the sleeves drooped. This was in case she had to hold the newborn babe.

*All slippery from spiraling down the birth canal!* It made

her giddy just thinking about such a possibility. She had, of course, not been alive two hundred years earlier when the unfortunate Prince Disaster had been born. Nor had anyone she knew.

*Except the queen. And the king.*

The king and queen of Faerie were always very long-lived. It was one of their privileges. Actually no one—maybe the minister of history—knew how old the king and queen really were.

*Well*, Snail thought, *I suppose* the king and queen *know*.

But everyone had heard about Prince Disaster. And everyone knew that she, Snail, was sometimes accident-prone. Why, Yarrow, that toffee-nosed suck-up, stuck-up apprentice to Mistress Yoke, had once laughed at her in front of all the midwives and said she had Dropitis and the Oopsies. Another time, at an apprentice party, she'd singled Snail out, saying to a pot boy, "Be careful around her, she's got slipshod fingers and careless hands and she *never* thinks ahead."

Snail shrugged. That was the way of it. Apprentices put other apprentices down. It was how they were able to curry favor and rise in rank. Even so-called friends whispered behind one another's backs, traded secrets, told tales.

*At least I don't do that.*

She wasn't actually sure she had any talent for midwifery. *Or, for that matter, anything else.* But she knew it wasn't from lack of trying. She knew that she was no stranger to mistakes. Like any apprentice, she'd fumbled a time or three.

She shook her head. *Be honest. All right, I've fumbled more than that. With things like dishes, spoons, bottles, and ham bones.* But she'd never dropped a baby.

Not ever.

Not . . . yet.

Though of course, she'd only actually handled three. The first was a dark-skinned, red-eyed drow infant, screaming and clawing as it came out into the light. The second had been the ostler's child who was part horse and part fey, with an ability to kick as soon as it was free from its sac. The third was a mermaid's newborn, the fish part of him wet and slippery. She hadn't dropped that one, either.

But what if she dropped the prince?

*Or the princess.*

She sighed aloud. *It* could *be a princess, though nobody wants one. They already have three of those, and two of them are twinned, haughty, stuck-up . . .* She shook her head. *Well, that's not much different than the other royals, really.*

She smoothed down the sleeves of her dress, and took a brush to her hair, beating it into submission. *Perhaps,* she thought, *perhaps Mistress Softhands should have named* me *Disaster, and not Snail.*

Making a mistake in the queen's birthing room—with its stark white walls and its large, high bed—carried more consequence than making a mistake in the birth cave of an ogre. After all, ogres were no longer allowed to eat midwives or their apprentices, a rule Snail had more than once been comforted by. But the queen—the queen could do anything she wished. And if someone made a mistake involving her newborn child, her wish could be very brutal and very swift.

Being eaten by an ogre, Snail thought, might actually be a preferable fate.

Snail suddenly remembered that no one ever spoke of the midwife who'd been in attendance when Prince Disaster had been delivered. No one mentioned her apprentice either. *That very silence*, Snail thought uneasily, *means something*. Thinking about it made her tremble.

She looked down at her traitorous, shaking hands and whispered, "That's the last thing I need, wobbly hands!"

*This is not*, she was sure of it, *going to be a good day*.

But she had to go to the kitchen to get something to eat. Mistress Softhands always cautioned, *Never deliver babies on an empty stomach*. Because, Snail knew, sometimes it takes many hours for a baby to appear and mistakes driven by hunger or thirst could often occur.

Her stomach continued to warn her that she'd eaten too much the night before. It was an argument she didn't dare lose. Instead, she ignored it and left the room without even making her bed, which she knew would almost certainly win her another telling-off.

Going quickly to the stairs, she headed for the kitchen below. She'd make an appearance and grab something small to stick in a pocket of her apron, something to eat later on, when her stomach was quieter.

The sounds of the kitchen on a feast day drifted up to meet her: clanging pots and chopping knives, the spits turning with a loud whirring noise. There were kettles boiling merrily and the shouts of cooks barking instructions to their apprentices, who shouted back at them. Cook boys and cook girls got away with sass that the midwife apprentices never dared.

All four ovens must have been in use, for the heat nearly drove her right back up the stairs. But she sneaked a quick peek in to see what might be on offer.

"Here at last, Mistress Drop-Everything." It was Yarrow, sitting like a lady at the cook's own table, acting as if she owned the kitchen. Her hair, unlike Snail's, was pulled back in a sedate black bun. Beside her sat the newest apprentice midwife, hand over mouth, giggling. She was one of those poor creatures whose only way of advancement was to toady up to a more successful girl and do her bidding, laugh at her jokes, fetch and carry without complaint.

*And she does it very well*, Snail thought.

Yarrow went on relentlessly, her narrow lips in a sneer that did not destroy her beauty. In fact, it enhanced it.

*Some toff*, Snail thought, *will soon notice her, some princeling or duke. And soon enough she will leave midwifery behind. She'll be renamed Star or Moonbeam or Sunshine, and eat in the Hall.*

"Well, you didn't drop things fast enough to get down here in time, and breakfast is already served, eaten, and digesting properly. And . . ." Yarrow turned and smiled that namby-pamby, peely-wally smile at the journeymen cooks around her, all of whom seemed to melt under the heat of her simper. If the journeymen cooks had a vote, Yarrow would have forthwith been elevated to a full midwife, despite the fact that—to Snail's certain knowledge—she had little intuition about a laboring woman's danger and less patience with the poor woman's complaints than a midwife needs. "And—" She made a jab toward Snail with a long fork, as if she knew Snail hated being poked in the belly.

Even that far away from the fork and in no danger of being poked with it, Snail flinched. She almost yelled at Yarrow, but bit back the response. She knew that fighting Yarrow spit for spite would win her nothing in this company, except that then everyone would know about her hating to be poked, so she bit her lip and didn't answer back. Instead she edged toward the barrel where the good leftovers were kept, ready to send out with the swine boy for his pigs.

"Away there, Snail!" hissed Nettle, one of the pot boys, and as close to a friend as she had. "No pinching food today."

As usual, his thatch of hair stuck straight up from his head as if permanently startled. It never needed any of the goop or goo or oil the other boys used to give them that banty-rooster hair.

Nettle looked perky today, not green or wan, though Snail definitely remembered him eating much more cake than she had last night. It seemed unfair. A few of the other apprentices in the kitchen looked as haggard from their long night's party as Snail felt. But there was Nettle grinning and pink-faced, clutching a huge haunch of raw venison to his chest and staggering toward the spits with it. As it was one of the finer pieces of meat in the kitchen, Snail knew that it was destined to be roasted with savory herbs and served to the High Court. The lesser pieces would be thrown into the stew pots for the rest of the guests. But raw—that was how the Border Lords liked theirs. Raw and still bleeding— like their enemies, as they proclaimed at every feast. Usually while banging their tankards loudly on the table.

"Why no pinching?" Snail asked, suddenly thinking, *Maybe it's a good thing I ate so much cake last night.* Her stomach seemed to congratulate her for the thought.

Nettle nodded his head to where a huge, squat creature perched on a high stool in the center of the room. "Bonetooth hisself is here today." Then he was off, maneuvering through the crowd of kitchen workers with his bloody burden.

Snail sighed and shifted her aim for the far doors of the kitchen, rather than the pantries. She needed to stay out of sight. Master Chef Bonetooth brooked no nonsense in his domain—and no latecomers or visitors! It was said that he got his cooking skills from his mother, a brownie who'd kept the kitchens in Dunvegan Castle for a hundred years, drinking milk from silver bowls left for her by the island chiefs themselves. While that may or not have been true, everyone *knew* that he got his temperament from his father.

An ogre.

Ducking and scampering to keep bodies between her and Bonetooth's line of sight, she was just passing the door into the Great Hall when disaster struck.

*Disaster always comes at the end*, Mistress Softhands liked to say, meaning that once disaster came, nothing else was ever the same.

Turning for a lingering a glance at a sideboard covered in soft cheeses and fresh bread, Snail failed to notice either the newest apprentice midwife sneaking behind her, nor the serving girl with a tray full of hot violet tea by her right elbow.

Suddenly, she felt a sharp shove in the small of her back, and cried out, "What are you . . ."

The girl behind her giggled.

The journeymen cooks wahooed.

Nettle cried out, "Snail!"

But it was too late. Snail crashed against the server, and they both fell through the doors into the Great Hall.

As they tumbled to the floor, the tray went sailing end over end. The teapot dropped, tea splattered, and Snail found herself looking up at a set of fine silken breeches that had, until very recently, been a beautiful shade of periwinkle. She looked up past the spreading stain on the left leg, past a green tunic to a white silken shirt with periwinkle threading and a slight spattering of purplish tea, to a clenched jaw and a pale face with high cheekbones that was framed by long, pointed ears.

*Oh, Puck*, Snail thought, horrified. This was almost as bad as making a mistake in the birth chamber. *I've spattered a noble.*

She reached her hands toward the toff, then stopped, holding them stupidly midway between rubbing at the stains and dropping them back in her lap.

*I'm no laundress. What if rubbing the stains makes them worse?* Then she thought, *What does it matter. I'm dead either way.*

She should have been terrified. But instead she was angry.

*That stupid girl has killed me. I'll never get to hold a royal babe.*

She suddenly realized that she'd actually been looking forward to holding the new prince. Or princess. She couldn't remember the last time she'd looked forward to something, and that thought made her even angrier.

She turned her anger on the nearest thing to her, glaring at the noble she'd spilled the tea on. If she'd given it a moment's thought, she would never have dared to do any such thing.

## PRINCE ASPEN REGRETS

$\mathcal{P}$rince Aspen watched the girls tumble and heard the teapot and cups shatter on the stone floor, only slightly softened by the rushes, but he didn't feel the spatters of tea on his well-lined silken breeches or his shirt. Only when some of it soaked through his sleeve was he aware of the heat.

Glancing down at the two girls sprawled at his feet, he saw that one was a midwife's apprentice. He knew her by her starched white apron and striped dress and the ghastly striped hose. He remembered that once the twin princesses Sun and Moon had remarked about a passing midwife that if a baby wasn't ready to come out on its own, all the midwife had to do was a shake a leg at it and the "horrible hose," as they called them, would frighten the baby into dropping down.

Unaccountably, the midwife's apprentice was glaring up at him. *Glaring,* though he was the injured party here, and she being a servant, of no importance at all.

He drew his hand back to strike her because that was

what was expected of him, and then he looked into her eyes. Truly looked. Astonishingly, one eye was green and one blue. He'd never seen anything like it. Fey eyes were always blue—not the blue of robin's eggs or the blue of running water, but the blue of a spring sky after a good soaking rain.

His hand was still uplifted and the other members of the High Court had gone silent, waiting to hear the sound of the slap on the girl's face and to drink in the sound she made in response, probably a whimper, possibly a cry. They would feast on the coloration of her cheek and the bruise after.

But his hand didn't move. He was mesmerized by her two-color eyes, and her cockscomb hair, an odd shade of red. They made him smile. And then laugh. His laughter was high-pitched still, his voice unbroken, although he was already fourteen and well past the time when it should have changed. He hadn't meant to laugh. He knew he'd regret it. Probably get nicknamed Prince Hee-Haw or something.

He had a collection of such names already. But he couldn't help himself. The girl's eyes were funny. *She* was funny. Should be helpless and frightened, head-bowed and shaking, and yet here she was, glaring up at him. He shrugged slightly at her to let her know he meant no harm, but no one else could tell, of that he was sure.

Aspen whispered, "Get up. Get up and get out of here. Do not stop to ask why. Now!"

She got up, bowed, moved swiftly, never turning her back

on any of them, which would be inviting death. And then she was gone. The other girl must have left almost immediately after dropping the tray.

Aspen knew it was a mistake when the laughter expanded all around the Great Hall, the Border Lords laughing loudest of all. But he found he couldn't regret it.

*Probably will, though*, he thought. *Later.*

"PRINCE Aspen!" A loud, familiar voice cut through the laughter. "And have we not taught you better in all this time with us?" It was his foster father, King Obs. Obs of the Hard Hand, as he was called, and his right hand was not only hard but huge. It was the size, someone once said, of a roasting platter. There were whispers that there had been a troll somewhere in the far back of his ancestry. But no one ever said such things aloud. "Your family will not thank us. They will say you are a tortoise, not taught at all."

*For a king's witticism*, Aspen thought, *that's pretty lame.* But then no one ever said this king was the brightest spark in the fire that was the Unseelie Court. Perhaps another gift of his troll ancestry. *Still, they'll all call me Tortoise now.*

He could live with it. He'd lived with all the other names.

In the seven years he'd been at the Unseelie Court as a princely hostage, guaranteeing peace between their two nations—just like the Unseelie prince languishing in his father's court—Aspen had been called too many names to remember. The only ones he truly regretted were the ones given to him by Princesses Sun and Moon, twins he'd loved from the moment he'd met them, though they were as far out of his reach as if they were truly the sun and the moon. They'd called him Little Bit, and Weeper, and Sniveler, and Fidget, all things he'd regrettably done in their presence, though mostly as a child. But amongst the fey, first impressions last a long, long time.

A lifetime.

Centuries.

"Slow and steady, your majesty," he called out to the king. "And wearing a very hard shell. Repels all splatters and shatters." *Not to mention names*, but he didn't say that out loud.

"Will you excuse her then?" asked the king, his voice thundering but his face clear of anger.

The Border Lords started banging the bone handles of their great knives on the table, causing all of the goblets to wobble. "NO EXCUSES! NO EXCUSES!" Several of them were drooling wine into their beards or spitting out the crumbs of something recently eaten. The usual.

With a wave of his huge right hand, King Obs silenced them. "Speak, Tortoise," he said. On either side of the king, the Unseelie princes leaned forward to hear Aspen's response. The Heir on the right—hefty, pockmarked and gap-toothed. On the left, the Spare—lean and listless. Their pasty faces wore smiles like a chimera's, all teeth and hunger, but their father's rough intelligence was missing.

"Excuse and accuse are two sides of the same coin,"

Aspen said, quoting one of the old Unseelie philosophers he'd recently been studying.

He nodded at Jaunty, his tutor, sitting way down at the far end of the room, and the old hob smiled at him, a green, toothy smile. "I excuse *both* the girls. They are hardly worth accusing."

King Obs applauded at that, his smaller left hand beating against the larger right, and the rest of the court took it up till the room shook with the noise. The two princes clapped greedily, as if they had been the ones to coin the witticism.

"In honor of the upcoming birth of my child, I accept your excuse. They are both spared. But do not be so quick next time to let such misbehavior go or the underfolk will take advantage of it. And what do you say to that?"

Aspen thought, and then he had it. *A warrior's response.* The king would like that. "They cannot take advantage, sire, because we princes have the high ground!"

"Hah!" The king's head went back with laughter, like a flower on a stalk finding the sun. He laughed so hard, his striped beard waggled, like a black-and-white flag.

The court began applauding with a steady beat, the kind that showed both appreciation and approval. All except for the twins, who only moved their long, beautiful pointer fingers in time to the beat.

But for Aspen, it was praise enough. He smiled. He didn't know it, but the smile changed his entire aspect. Made him look younger, nicer, more common. Had he known, he would have hated it. Would never smile again.

"Come, boy, sit," the king said.

Aspen bowed his head and sat.

"Bring on the food," the king commanded. And the room sprang to life as servers once again appeared as if by magic, carrying in haunches of beeves, ducks and pheasants stuffed with grains, eels soaked in vinegar. They brought in cheeses rolled in oats, and loaves of crusty braided bread, as well as roasted potatoes and seven kinds of salad leaves soaked in oil and dashed with herbs. And without even waiting for any courses to be finished—*as if you could call any of this chaos a course*, Aspen thought—they brought in plate after plate of gigantic sugary puddings.

The Unseelie did love their sweets.

As the servers bustled around them, Aspen drew in a deep breath. He thought it barely audible with all the noise from the food being brought in. But up the table from him, Sun and Moon snickered, and Aspen knew it was about him. The sound was not beautiful coming from two such beautiful young women, but he didn't care. It made him love them the more. And that was what he regretted most of all.

"You'd do just as well to worship the actual celestial bodies as those two," said Old Jack Daw, appearing next to Aspen's seat in a swirl of black robes and giving Aspen a shallow bow. "A hundred years and they have learned little."

Jack was a drow, a creature as much carrion bird as man, and the king's senior counselor. Despite his advanced age, he was the closest thing Aspen had to a friend in the Dark Court. Even more than Jaunty, he had taught Aspen how to survive his Unseelie exile. And he'd done it out of friendship, not because the king had assigned him to the job.

"Your Serenity," Jack added, then looked at the king. Long, dark ears nearly pointing at the ground, Jack bowed much more deeply to the king than he had to Aspen. Then, pulling up a rickety stool next to Aspen, he snatched a slice of meat off a passing tray.

Aspen caught a whiff of decay as the old drow popped the meat into his mouth. *Must have been a slice destined for the ogres' table. They like their meat uncooked and half rotten.* "I know the twins are far above my shallow skies," he said petulantly. He looked down at his still-empty plate. "I am not a fool."

Jack chewed rapidly. "By your display with the serving girl—"

Without thinking, Aspen corrected the old drow. "Midwife's apprentice."

Jack gave him a look that would have curdled milk on a baby's tongue. "As I said, by your display with the . . . girl . . . I might argue the point. Mercy—"

"Is not highly prized here," Aspen finished for him, again without thought. "I know. You have been telling me that ever since I arrived."

"And yet you still haven't taken the lesson." With a sharp black fingernail, Jack dug a piece of gristle from between two of his few remaining teeth. "You have been listening to that silly old fool Jaunty when you should have been listening to me." He peered at the gristle as if interested in its history. "Perhaps it's true that you can take a Seelie lord out of his court but you can't make him Unseelie. You are soft, boy. Too soft." He licked his lips swiftly, once, with a thin forked tongue the same drab grey as his skin. "And you need to learn when to keep silent. Oh, not for the way you speak to me. That is as it should be. You are a lord, and I . . ." He hesitated. Maybe even changed his mind about what he was about to say. Then said, "I am not."

Aspen thought it showed wisdom on the drow's part. Or craft. He wasn't sure which.

"But enough of lessons you refuse to heed. Lord Bloody-Knives-and-Kneecaps has brought me news from the borders." He flicked the gristle to the floor and motioned Aspen in closer. "News not fit for all ears."

Aspen leaned in despite the ghastly odor of Jack's breath. "What news?"

"Nothing good," Jack whispered. "Your father's armies mass there. War may almost be upon us."

"He wouldn't!" Aspen cried.

"Quiet, boy!" Jack hissed. "He may be pushed to it. The Border Lords are raiding nightly. And they do not stop at mere cattle thieving. There's the occasional dead lord and violated lady and children roasted on a spit. The truce is hanging by a spider's thread."

Aspen shuddered at the news. "And if the truce is broken . . ." He felt a line of perspiration start to meander between his shoulder blades.

Jack drew a spindly finger across his neck. "The hostages will be the first casualties."

Aspen pushed his still-empty plate away. One of the problems with sitting this far from the king's table was that a person might never get served. "You mean *I* will be the first casualty." He was not only their most important hostage, he was—as far as he knew—their *only* hostage. Though he supposed there could always be one secreted away in the dungeon or in a pigsty. He wouldn't put that past the king.

Or the queen.

"Yes, my boy," Jack said solemnly. "You will be the first casualty of the Seelie Wars. As will the Unseelie prince hostage in your father's hall."

"Yes, *Your Serenity*," Aspen reminded the old drow, though his heart was not in it. He was wondering instead why Jack had said *wars* in the plural.

Jack leaned in again to whisper, his carrion breath hot on Aspen's ear. "But do not despair yet! Lord Bloody is not the most reliable of my sources. More news will probably come tomorrow and may set all to ease." He reached across and pulled Aspen's plate back.

Now the plate was filled with food, a glop of gravy and pieces of nearly raw meat plus something grey that was once green. Aspen felt his stomach turn over.

"But if not," Jack added, "you had best eat. You will need your strength."

Aspen looked at food which had somehow made an appearance on his plate, and sighed. It might as well have been made of paste and mud. He was definitely *not* hungry now.

"To do what? I do not think any amount of strength will keep my head from being separated from my shoulders once war actually breaks out." He tried for a kind of wry resignation, the way the older princes spoke, with a casual shrug. It came out instead in a childish whine. He hated that.

Jack smiled kindly, an odd expression on such a wizened, grey face, but Aspen knew it was genuine. "You are dear to me, boy. I will not let you come to harm so easily."

"Thank you, Jack. I . . ." Aspen stopped short, suddenly afraid he would burst into tears if he tried to say anything more. Princely honor—both Seelie and Unseelie—demanded that he face everything with aplomb and grace, whether it was murder, war, or simply tea that had gone a bit cold.

*Though not*, he thought suddenly, *if something was done by an underling that undermined authority or honor.*

Aspen squared his shoulders and looked directly at Jack. He'd done his best for every day of the seven years he'd been at the Unseelie Court, alone amongst his enemies, to do just that, to be careful and honorable. But the thought of being executed made him remember how young and scared he really was. And no amount of royal dignity could change that.

"Your Serenity," Old Jack Daw said, his eyes sparkling with emotion. "I am a simple servant, and you are a Lord of the Realm. Save your thanks for someone more deserving."

It was the kind of overdone courtesy one used with a higher-ranking courtier, not with a friend. Aspen needed the friend more. He forced a smile. It felt like it might even stick. "And my mercy?"

Jack grinned, courtesy forgotten. "Do not waste any more of it on serving girls or midwives' apprentices! Let King Obs know how valuable you really are."

"Done!" Aspen said. And to prove he belonged in the company of those around him, he grabbed the nearest serving girl roughly and shoved her toward the kitchen. "More meat for Old Jack Daw! And be quick about it, or we will pop *you* in the ovens next!"

The Border Lords roared their approval and flung their dishes at the poor girl's heels to hurry her along, before turning back to bang upon the table with the butt ends of their knives once more and shouting a praise song to Aspen that tried to rhyme his name with *grasping* and failed.

Glancing up from his tankard at the noise, King Obs grinned at Aspen.

Even the twins looked down the table at him with something like approval on their beautiful, enigmatic faces.

Strangely, it didn't make Aspen feel as good as he thought it would.

He picked a piece of fruit from a nearby bowl and took a big, juicy bite. *Dust,* he thought. *It tastes like dust and decay. And death.*

But he ate it with gusto anyway, because *that* was what Unseelie princes always do.

# SNAIL IN THE TOWER ROOM

*B*y the time Snail got back into the kitchen, she was shaking. At first she thought it was from fear, but she soon realized it was from anger. Even more anger than before. For now, heaped onto that earlier anger, was this new offense.

How that toff, that stupid prince had glared at her and made a face, as if seeing some piece of donkey dung stuck to the bottom of one of his silken shoes. And then he'd shouted at her to "get up and get out of here! Do not stop to ask why." And dismissed her without even asking if she'd been injured in the fall.

*And the way those toffs talk*, she thought. *"Do not," instead of "don't." "Cannot" instead of "can't."* As if plain talk wasn't good enough for them.

Not that she expected a prince would concern himself with her feelings and her way of speaking. Their kind never did. Not princes. Not like real folk.

"A fall," she said aloud, "that was no fault of my own." She looked around to see if she could find who'd pushed her into the serving girl who then had dropped the platter with the teapot and cups. "If I find you, you'll get an earful, I promise you that!" *And maybe more.*

Nettle came over and handed her a twist of second-day cheese bread and a cup of water. "Here. Now, better make yourself scarce. Old Bonetooth has already chewed up that hapless serving girl and spit out the pips, and he won't make no distinction between you being a midwife's apprentice or the girl who carried the dropped tray."

"But someone pushed me . . ." she began.

"No blame, no shame," he said.

"What do you mean . . ." she started to say and then stopped. Because suddenly she knew. The one to blame was Yarrow, of course, who must have told the new girl to give her a shove. They were probably both giggling over it upstairs. But no one would back Snail on this because of how besotted the potboys were with Yarrow.

Snail looked around. Yarrow and the other girl were already gone from the room. The serving girl who'd dropped the tray was nowhere to be seen, probably cowering in a cupboard somewhere.

Suddenly she noticed that Master Chef Bonetooth was running a bloody cloth across his lips. "He *ate* her?"

Such a punishment wasn't unheard of, of course. But those sort of things happened only in the Seelie Court.

*Not here*, Snail thought.

Suddenly all her anger left her and she began to tremble

in a different way. Her legs felt as if they were wobbling, and she doubted her knees would hold her up much longer.

"Scarce!" Nettle repeated, pointing toward the door.

Grateful that she had such a friend in Nettle, she was through the door before he could say another word, collapsing on the other side. And there she lay on the floor, trying to catch not only her breath but her courage, which seemed to be running away from her faster than a will-o'-the-wisp on a summer's eve.

Suddenly someone grabbed her shoulder from behind. Snail flinched and hunched her shoulders. *I will not cry, I will not cry,* she told herself. *He may chew me up, but I will not cry!*

In fact, she was too frightened to cry.

"There you are. Where've you been, you silly girl? You'll have to go and wash up all over again. Floor's not the place for a midwife's apprentice that's got to be cleaner than clean. Especially right now."

Snail looked over her shoulder into Mistress Softhands's red face. "I thought you were Chef Bonetooth," she stuttered, "come to eat . . . eat . . . *eat* me." She took a deep breath. "And chew me to bits."

"Slovenly—and stupid as well, are you? He's his mother's son. Milk and cheese is all that one gobbles down, don't you know."

"Really?" She searched the old midwife's face for some sense of a joke. But her face was as humorless as ever.

"The only ogre you have to worry about is one in a birthing chamber."

"I thought there was a law against them eating midwives."

"I always knew you were quick, the quickest of all the apprentices, so use that nog of yours. And stand up!" Mistress Softhands stood, arms folded, watching her.

*I am?* Snail was stunned, but was quick enough for the moment not to say it aloud. Instead, she got up slowly until she was sure her still-shaking legs would hold. She felt a stone lift from her belly. "That Nettle!" she said with some passion, fists clenched at her side. "I'll kill him, I will!"

"Ah, well, if you take the word of someone called Nettle," her mistress said, holding Snail's face in her hand and shaking her right finger, "then you deserve every rash and sting you get." Then she turned away from Snail, but not before saying over her shoulder, "Now quick. The queen's time is here, and none too soon by the looks of her. I've been telling Mistress Yoke for weeks, we should have been slipping her beth root to make the baby come sooner. Of the nine midwives, I've been the only one concerned. Now she's well over her time and it will just make things harder. And you know what they say about cross queens."

Snail thought, *Sooner a hungry dragon than a cross queen.*

"Has she really begun at last?" was all she dared to ask.

Luckily Mistress Softhands was distracted enough by the work ahead not to scold her about this, saying only, "Of course, of course. Why else would I be in such a pother!

Now go wash and meet me at the birthing tower quicker than quick." And off she went, as fast as if she'd a magic witch broom between her legs.

The thought of Mistress Softhands on such an instrument of travel almost made Snail laugh out loud, but she held it in. She'd already gotten into enough trouble for one day.

❖ ❖ ❖

SNAIL WENT INTO the nearest washing chamber and cleaned up from her twin spills on the floor—*the tumble and the crumple*, as she called them to herself. After that, she went up to her bedchamber and put on a fresh, starched apron. The dress and the hose seemed surprisingly clean.

A quick inspection in the small mirror and she was off down the hall and then three stairways up to the Great Tower, where the queen was to give birth.

Of course, the queen was not there yet. She was in her great bed in the chamber next door, lying down. In between the birth pains she played cards with her ladies—Knaves High and Split the River, real ladies' games, not the kind of cutthroat games the servants played below stairs like Pinch, Poke Her, and Hold Them Down. When not calling out her cards, the queen was shouting out orders. Snail was not allowed in the queen's bedchamber—only a master midwife could go in to check on her—but Snail could hear her bellowing easily enough, even through the heavy wooden door. The queen might be delicate as a wren and as lovely as a hummingbird, as the minstrels sang, but no one ever said she had a soft voice.

"I want some of that sweet apple wine, now. *NOW,* you fool! Not later," the queen howled, and then added, "Oof, another one of those pains. Yes, by the green gods it hurts, and no, I will not sit up. YOU can sit up yourselves." Clearly this last was said to whichever midwife was examining her.

"Just LEAVE ME BE," the queen continued. "I have a hand to play. No. *NO!* Do not leave me, you stupid midwife. Do what I mean, not what I say. I want that WIIIIIIINE!"

Snail turned into the first of the three birthing chambers, the one where Mistresses Softhands, Yoke, and Treetop were in charge of Snail, Yarrow, and the new apprentice. The queen would not make a final decision as to which chamber to give birth in until the very last moment, nor which three of the nine midwives would be in attendance. It was a ploy to fool any wicked spirits or Seelie spies who might be wishing the new baby harm.

*And to make more work for us,* Snail thought, but didn't say so aloud. She just walked into the room, rolled up her sleeves, held her hands and arms out for Mistress Treetop to inspect. When the midwife nodded, Snail went over to the narrow bed and the mattress that she was to stuff with newly gathered Ladies' Bedstraw. The bedstraw would not only sweeten the air of the tower, but also ease the baby's passage into the light.

She saw Yarrow, Mistress Yoke's apprentice, already setting

out the juniper twigs, juniper berries, and seeds of the ash tree in the great hearth, forming them into circles of power. Yarrow was looking perfect as always, not a raven hair out of place.

*I should say something*, Snail thought. But then she realized it would give Yarrow another excuse to accuse her. And all the midwives would back Yarrow on that, since making disagreements or pother in a birthing room—and especially the queen's birthing room—was the worst sort of thing a midwife could do.

*All potheration set aside at the bedfoot*, Mistress Softhands always cautioned.

Yarrow would be lighting the herb piles soon and saying the words of cleansing. As the oldest of the apprentices, she'd had her choice of jobs. It was no surprise she left the gathering of hand towels, birth cloths, and such to the newest girl. Snail suddenly remembered her name—Philomel.

*Plenty of time after*, Snail thought, *to get back at the two of them. Maybe revenge really is best as cold soup rather than hot porridge, as the old saying goes.*

Stuffing the mattress appealed to Snail anyway. Fire-making was a precise task in the birthing room. If it went wrong, the whole tower could be filled with smoke, and everything would have to be moved to a lower chamber, including the queen on a litter.

*And if something can go wrong*, Snail knew, *it will go wrong, especially if I'm in charge.*

Suddenly, she was *very* glad all she had to do was stuff the mattress. Even if the bedstraw *was* prickly. She liked the smell, and the ordinariness of the task. She began to hum to herself, one of the songs the pot boys had been singing at last night's party.

> *And she winked,*
> *And he blinked,*
> *And their hearts both beat as one . . .*

It was a tune that caught up in one's ear. A ballad about a changeling who changed a prince's heart. The song helped her move the bedstraw into the coverlet in an even, flowing motion.

Mistress Softhands came by and swatted her on the head. "If you must sing, sing a song of queen's praise," she said. "Or a song of jubilation for the event at hand. None of this silly, common nonsense. A changeling can't never even *talk* to a prince. And singing such heresy in the queen's tower room? What are you *thinking*, child!"

Snail swallowed down her retort and began to hum the only praise song she knew. The words went something like, "Glorious queen . . . dum-ti-dum . . . ever been . . . dum-dum-ti-dum . . . in the highest . . ." *Oh, it has no joy in it. No fun. No proper smooth rhythm, either.* But not wanting to be swatted again, she stopped singing altogether, and just punched in handsful of the bedstraw until the mattress was lumpy and coarse.

"Look at what Snail's gone and done!" It was toffee-nosed Yarrow, standing over her and pointing.

The three midwives surrounded the bed, shaking their heads, *tsk*ing, shaking fingers, and looking dour as only midwives can amongst themselves on the day of a birth.

"I'll shake it out," Yarrow said, in that snooty way she had, and, with several quick flicks of her wrists, did just that.

"I was about to shake it down," said Snail, but no one heard her because just then the queen started bellowing again.

This time there were no words in what she was saying, just a lot of screams and whines, and an occasional roar.

Snail ran to the door but knew better than to throw it open. Unless there was a knock indicating the queen had chosen their room, it was punishable by death to do so. Instead, she stooped, put her eye to the keyhole, and looked into the chaos of the hall.

On a litter carried by four blinded trolls—trolls were not supposed to look at the queen if she was not perfectly dressed and glowing—the queen thrashed about, her slim arms waving, be-ringed hands clutching at the air. Her normally serene face was red and sweaty as a farmer's wife, and she was using words Snail had only heard the dog boys say, swears of such monumental force that Snail was surprised the air in the hallway hadn't turned blue or the stones in the tower melted and run like whey.

"Look at Snail!" Yarrow cried out from across the room. "She's spying! She's *spying*!" At the same time, she pushed Philomel, who darted forward to try and pull Snail from the door.

But Mistress Softhands shouted, "Leave her!" and bulled her way through the two hysterical girls, then leaned down over Snail's shoulder and whispered. "What do you see, girl?"

Snail was so surprised at that, she almost took her eye from the keyhole. But what she saw next so stunned her, she kept on looking.

## ASPEN'S DESPERATE PLAN

*A*spen excused himself from dinner as soon as was seemly and scurried to his apartment. He needed to be alone with his tumultuous thoughts.

*How could my father do this to me?* he thought, stomping back and forth in the main room.

Measuring twelve paces by ten, the room was small by princely standards, but no real insult to a king's younger son, and a hostage at that. It was well-appointed: an inglenook fireplace big enough to roast a pig in should he have desired, a fine oaken desk, cushioned chairs on a woven silk rug, the giant chest holding his prized garments. There were two windows with views across the great wall to the Downs. Aspen paced toward the fireplace till his face was hot, then turned to glare at the single worn tapestry that hung on the far wall. It depicted King Obs and his nobles in some unnamed victorious battle.

"Obs and the Mobs," Aspen called it, but only when he knew himself to be entirely alone.

He had told no one that name, not Jaunty, not Jack Daw, and—he felt a tremor go down his back—certainly not the twin princesses.

*It's not right. It's not fair.*

He stomped up to the tapestry until he could smell the stale, barnyard smell of the woolen threads and get a close-up view of the unrealistic muscles the artist had given the king. The king was skewering a fey lord who looked suspiciously like Aspen's father, or at least how he remembered his father.

*Serves Father right,* he thought. *First he sends me away, and then he starts a war. He'll get me killed, and then we'll probably lose the war anyway.*

The Border Lords alone were a match for anything he could remember from his childhood in the Seelie Court. And they weren't even the worst creatures King Obs had at his command. He had trolls and ogres and bloodyguts and Red Caps and the Wild Hunt and . . .

He paced back toward the fire. *Of course, I don't know why I say "we." I've been here so long, I'm probably more Un than Seelie.* He stopped suddenly in the middle of the room.

"And that might very well save me!"

He ran out of the room and back down the great stairs to the feast.

❖ ❖ ❖

Now it was less of a feast and more of a drunken revel. Aspen never understood the older lords' fascination with liquor.

*Even if you start the evening clever and well-spoken, you end it as an ignorant lout,* he thought. *And Oberon help you if you were an imbecile to begin with!*

King Obs, while not the sharpest sword in a sheath, was neither ignorant nor imbecilic, yet judging by how far he was leaning over the table and the low level of mead in his bowl, Aspen feared he was well on his way to becoming both.

*Maybe I should ask at another time.* But before he could turn to leave, the king saw him and called out.

"Prince Tortoise! Approach me." His voice was a low rumble, which in itself was ominous.

Cursing his own bad luck, Aspen said, "Of course, sire," and waded through the crowd toward the king.

When he reached the throne, he took a knee and bowed his head. "Yes, sire?"

King Obs patted him clumsily on the head. "Look at you, Tortoise. Always so respectful. So polite. Always such a *good* boy."

When he said *good*, it didn't sound like a compliment.

"Thank you, sire," Aspen replied. It was what one always said to a king, whether he was praising you or cursing you.

"What am I to do with you should I ever go to war with your father?"

With the king so far in his cups, Aspen hadn't thought it was the right time to talk to him about his new idea. But now the king had asked a direct question.

*And Old Jack always says the best way to convince someone to do something is to make him think it's his own idea.*

"Well, sire, I had been giving that some thought actually." He was speaking too swiftly, words tumbling one after the other, and he forced himself to stop and take a breath. Strange, given what he was about to ask, but it was his father's voice he heard when he thought, *You are a prince of the Fair Folk. Act like one!*

"And?" King Obs asked, one bleary eye focused on Aspen, the other peering at the now-empty bottom of his mead bowl. Not something the ordinary fey could do.

"Sire," Aspen said, more calmly this time, "I have lived here longer than I lived at my father's court. I can barely remember my father's face, let alone that of any of my siblings." It wasn't entirely the truth, but it wasn't entirely a lie, either. He'd forgotten old Lisbet's face, and she'd been dearer to him than his father, or most of his siblings. She'd even packed him clothes enough to carry him into adulthood, wrapping them within precious paper on which she'd printed instructions in her peasant script to the laundress on how to take proper care.

He took a deep, slow breath and continued. "My life there is a distant and not particularly fond memory." He lifted his chin, determined to look directly into whichever eye was looking at him. Surprisingly, King Obs seemed to have sensed something important was coming, and had both eyes on him now, clear and focused.

"Sire, I request that you adopt me as a noninheriting son and allow me to stay here." Aspen had to force himself not to gulp visibly before the next word. "Forever."

*It's better than death,* he reminded himself.

King Obs sat perfectly still, eyes locked with Aspen's for just long enough for the young prince to fear that the king had fallen asleep with his eyes open. Then the king smiled. It was not a pleasant smile. But then he never smiled pleasantly. It wasn't the Unseelie way.

"Wouldn't that just make the pious old fart eat his own spleen!"

Aspen forced a smile. "I suppose that is an extra bonus, sire."

"Come closer, boy." King Obs reached out and took Aspen by the arm with a meaty hand. "I shall certainly consider it."

"Thank you, sire." Aspen bowed his head, trying to decide whether to feel relief or revulsion.

"It won't save you if it comes to war, you know," the king said.

Aspen couldn't help himself this time. *Gulp.* "Why not?"

"Look around you." The king turned Aspen to face the room, still full of Unseelie revelers. "Trolls, boggarts, drows, bogies—do you think they follow me out of love? Respect? Honor? Duty? Do you think Red Caps care about all of that? Or the Border Lords? Or the ogres? Or the Wild Hunt?"

Dismally, Aspen shook his head. He was afraid he knew where this was going.

"No, my young prince. It's fear and fear alone that keeps their spears at my command and their daggers in their belts instead of my back." He spun Aspen back around and pulled him close. His breath smelled of honey mead and rotten meat. "If I show a moment's mercy, a moment's weakness, they will tear me apart."

The king released Aspen's arm, and Aspen stumbled as he realized his legs had gone weak and the king had basically been holding him up.

"But, sire, if I were your *son*—"

"No," the king interrupted. "Son or no, you would die at the first clash of swords between our kingdoms."

"But why?"

"Because I swore an oath you would." King Obs thumped his bowl on the table and a servant scuttled forward to brim it with golden mead. The king took a healthy draught and wiped his mouth with his sleeve. "And a king keeps his word, no matter the consequences. You'd do well to keep that in mind, *Prince*."

Aspen nodded mutely, beyond words now.

The king waved his hand, dismissing him. "I shall give

your request due thought and give you my answer soon. Now off with you. I'll not have anyone of your young age— whether my son or the son of my greatest enemy—see what the Border Lords get up to when they're into their tenth bowl of mead."

Aspen turned on numb legs and staggered out of the Great Hall.

*Only an hour ago I was condemned to die. Now I'm to die as the son of my family's enemy.* Now even if war didn't come he had no hope of ever going home. He was stuck here at the Unseelie Court. Forever. Or as long as it took to hear the first horn of the first Seelie War.

He cursed himself for believing any thought or plan of his could do anything but make things worse.

But a worse thought quickly followed.

*If I run, then the truce is broken and I will be responsible for the death of thousands and as such will be a hunted man in both kingdoms.*

For the second time in just a few moments, he cursed himself for a fool.

*If there's going to be a war anyway, then running won't be the cause. Old Jack will bring me the news before he brings it to the king. That I'm sure of! He's a good man, Jack Daw. Well, a good drow anyway. And then once war is declared, if I can escape, and make it to the Seelie Court, I will be a hero.*

*Yes,* he thought, there would be a window, a brief one,

but a window nonetheless. Once he could be certain there was to be a war, but before the king locked down his hostage and prepared for the execution, those few hours would be his only chance.

*That's when I'll make my escape.*

Aspen went up the stairs two at a time, legs suddenly strong again. But this time he didn't go to his apartments to pace. This time he went to prepare.

# SNAIL SPIES THE QUEEN'S HALLWAY

*O*ut in the queen's hallway one of the blind trolls, normally so sensitive even to a bit of dust on the floor, slipped. Perhaps it was because the queen was screaming and tossing about on the bed. Perhaps it had to do with the heat in the tower. Or the way the new moon sat cradled in the old moon's arms.

*Or perhaps*—Snail thought—*my bad luck is catching. It is, after all, the third tumble of the day.* Then she had another thought and would have smiled if there'd been anything to smile about. *Though, luckily enough, this time the bad luck is not mine.*

Turning, she said, in a scared, hush voice, "She's stumbled."

"What?" All three midwives spoke as one. "Who?"

"The right forward troll," Snail whispered. "The one with the scar across her nose. She's down on one huge knee."

"Let me see!" hissed Philomel, poking Snail in the belly with a finger and pushing her unceremoniously aside.

"Hey!" Snail said, still hardly above a whisper. She'd all but doubled up, not with pain but with revulsion. *No one,* she thought, *pokes me in the belly!* She was about to say something more when she saw Mistress Softhands shake her head and put a finger to her lips.

Philomel noticed none of this in her eagerness to get to the keyhole. Yarrow crowded in as well, and Snail had to scurry on her bottom like a Ness crab to escape being stomped on.

Mistress Softhands shot Snail a look of pity, but turned quickly back to Philomel, who was busy fending off Yarrow, who was trying to secure the keyhole from her.

"Leave off, Yarrow!" said Mistress Softhands in a harsh whisper, as Mistresses Yoke and Treetop joined her to the side of the door. Then to Philomel, "Tell us what you see."

Philomel put her eye back to the hole, gasped, and said— much too loudly and with a crow of astonishment—"There are two of 'em down now. Fat old things."

In her excitement—not only at the illicit viewing, but also at the undivided attention and approval of all three midwives— Philomel forgot to whisper. In fact, she practically screeched the last three words.

*Fat. Old. Things.*

The queen must have heard and thought the keyhole was criticizing her weight, for she'd gained a pound or three with the child. Sitting up in the bed, she stopped screaming and lifted her right hand into the sudden silence.

All this Philomel dutifully reported in her increasingly

too-loud voice, as if she believed the door kept her every utterance a secret from the queen.

"Golly, she's big!" said Philomel, maybe meaning the troll, maybe meaning the queen. It was unclear to all of them.

It was also the last thing she was ever to say.

Lightning—or the hot, blue, magical equivalent of lightning—streamed through the keyhole, lit Philomel up for a moment till she looked like a star, and then struck her dead.

The room rocked with thunder. Every bit of Yarrow's carefully arranged fire circles was scattered. The lumpy mattress slipped unaccountably through the arrow slit, landing four stories down in the garden below, though no one thought such a thing possible.

On one side of the door, Yarrow was lifted in the air and tossed the length of the room to hit the wall with an ugly thud.

On the other side the three midwives were treated the same. Only they didn't hit the wall.

They hit Snail.

All that saved her was that she managed to curl into a ball as the three sizable midwives hurtled at her. They squashed her against the wall and she lay still, trying to consider each individual bone, hoping nothing was broken. Finally, she came to the conclusion that everything was whole—with the possible exception of her pride.

But as no one dared move for long minutes, Snail was afraid

that having no broken bones wouldn't matter. Instead, she would certainly end up crushed. Together, the midwives weighed almost as much as any troll.

She wiggled a finger painfully. After a long minute, she was able to move her right arm a bit. Once that arm was free, she was able to shift to one side so that her left arm could move as well. At last, with two free arms, she was able to drag herself out from under the midwives, though she was immediately exhausted by the effort.

That was when she heard a strange sound—*like a pig in labor*, she thought—coming from across the room. She knew what laboring pigs sounded like. Apprentice midwives got to practice on them before being allowed into any fey birthing room.

Looking around, she realized it was Yarrow making the ghastly noise.

*Well, at least she's alive*, Snail thought. *I won't have to clean the whole room up myself.*

But even that thought was a bit unwelcome. Yarrow was now whimpering so loudly, Snail was sure the queen, with her supersensitive hearing, would strike again.

"Shhhh," Snail hissed at her. "Shhhhhh!" and pointed to the door.

Yarrow's whimpering moderated a bit but never stopped.

As nothing more was heard from the door, no more lightning through the keyhole, no ogres or Red Caps coming in to eat them whole, Snail got to her hands and knees.

She was pleased that—except for an extremely dirty pair of hands and her hair being all askew—she was fine. *Nothing broken, nothing torn, nothing past saving.*

She stood up slowly, then went over to the door, and knelt by poor Philomel's remains, though all that was left of her was a bit of dust and a silver locket.

Oddly, Snail felt a tear in her eye. She wiped it brusquely away.

*Hrmph!* she thought. *I hardly knew her, and what I did know I didn't much like.* But a push in the back didn't warrant such an awful end. Snail knew she'd wanted revenge, but not this. Not just a pile of dust in a cold room.

Another tear came and dripped down onto the silver locket. It sizzled and disappeared where it hit. Snail was glad she hadn't touched the thing. It obviously wasn't cool yet, or free of the queen's magic. Sometimes silver could hold the remnants of a spell for hours and even be dangerous a day later.

Wiping her eyes, she stood up.

*It's just this place. So much random pain and . . . and . . . meanness!* She thought of Nettle and his pranks. *Not on the same level as the queen's anger, of course. But still . . .*

She moved her right shoulder, which was beginning to stiffen up. Then, sighing, she turned back to look at the midwives. They seemed fine, if a bit shaken. Their eyes were wide open, watching her. But they didn't look like they dared move yet.

*Fine—lie there in a pile like sows after a feeding,* she thought. *But if I'm going to die, I'd rather it was while I was doing something.*

Not that there was much to do. The room had been destroyed, and wouldn't be suitable for *any* birthing, let alone the queen's.

She glanced down at the locket and dust. *There's nothing I can do for Philomel now.*

Hearing a whimper, she remembered Yarrow, and started toward her. "Are you all right?" she whispered when she got close.

She knew already the answer would be "No!" Yarrow's usual response to her, but she bent over to inspect her anyway. Snail could see that Yarrow's left foot was bruised and swelling—possibly not broken, but obviously badly injured. There was also a bump the size of a falcon's egg on her forehead, and it seemed to be growing fast.

Yarrow looked up at her, eyes struggling a bit to focus. Then she scrunched her forehead and spit at Snail, "This is all *your* fault!"

"How?" Snail gasped, straightening up in amazement. "How is this *my* fault?"

"You were spying first! If you hadn't been spying, she'd never have thought of it. She wasn't that bright. *You* got Philomel killed!"

Snail bit her lip. There was some truth in what Yarrow said.

"Yes!" Mistress Treetop called from the midwife pile. "You got my apprentice killed!"

Then Yoke struggled to her feet and scuttled over to her wounded apprentice. "There, there, my dear girl," she said, "we'll make sure that nasty Snail gets her comeuppance."

With a wrinkled, clawed hand she patted Yarrow's midnight hair.

"But I . . ." Snail could think of nothing to say in her own defense so she turned to Mistress Softhands in the hope of finding some support there. But her midwife was just staring at the door, as if somehow blaming *it* for all that had happened.

Slumping to the floor, Snail let the buzz of the three women all talking at once fade into a cicada's nighttime trill. They were blaming her for everything—from the troll's slipping to the queen's mood to the lightning through the door. It didn't help to listen further.

Snail felt like whimpering herself. Like her namesake, she'd begun to pull herself into a kind of shell, curling away from the others, when there was a sudden knock on the door.

Three raps, two, three. *The signal.* All unaccountably, and quite beyond reason, the queen had chosen their chamber.

Without giving it further thought, Snail went over and opened the door.

## ASPEN'S PACKED BAG

*A*spen looked dejectedly at the small pile of possessions on his bed. Aside from the traveling necessities—stout leather breeches, sturdy boots and socks, a woolen cloak, a pack stuffed with dried meat and hard biscuits, a tinderbox in case magic failed him in the Wild Woods—there was only his sword, a small skinning dagger, five letters he'd received from his mother over the years, the ink faded to near invisibility from numerous rereadings, and his old pillow toy.

*It's not much to show for seven years in a place,* he thought, picking a stray thread from the cloak thoughtfully. He shrugged and stood. *Well, I was planning on traveling light anyway.*

Scooping up the lot and pushing it into the pack, he shoved it under the bed, all the way to the center where a thousand years of dust had gathered.

*My father would never let a servant get away with that kind of laziness!* he thought.

But Unseelie laziness was a boon to Aspen now, as there was almost no chance of anyone accidentally coming upon his escape supplies and asking uncomfortable questions.

Changing into a sleeping shirt and cap, he closed the curtain and climbed into the large bed. He arranged the many pillows into a soft fortress to surround him, and then—despite his worries—he fell swiftly asleep. If he dreamed at all, he was never to remember it.

❖ ❖ ❖

HE WAS AWAKENED an unknowable amount of time later by a clawed hand shaking his shoulder softly. It was dark as a dungeon. Or as black as he assumed a dungeon was. He'd never actually been down to check the dungeons out.

"Your Serenity, you must wake!"

The voice was familiar.

Aspen opened one eye and squinted into the darkness. Two yellow ovals glowed at him. Jack Daw's eyes, like a hunting wolf's, reflected what little light shone through the now-uncovered window slit.

"Jack?" Aspen asked, then cursed himself for sounding young and afraid. He sat up, started again. "Explain yourself!" This time his voice was lower and—he hoped—more confident.

Jack leaned over the bed and moonlight through the window slit illuminated his grey face. "It *is* war," he said quietly.

"War," Aspen squeaked, no longer bothering to deepen his voice. "So soon? But I thought we had at least a season or, at worst, a few days. What now?"

"You must go." Jack began pulling pillows from the bed and tossing them to the floor. "Are you prepared?"

Aspen threw his legs over the side of the bed and rubbed his eyes once. He thought about the pack under the bed. Would it be enough? Too late to change it now. "Yes."

"Good lad."

Aspen didn't correct him.

"The Water Gate is open and a boat is waiting. The guards are . . . indisposed."

"Water Gate. Boat. Got it." Aspen stood, then knelt down, digging under the bed for his pack and the supplies, this time cursing the thick dust and holding back a sneeze.

"Good lad," Jack repeated. "You *are* prepared. That makes things easier. The river will take you south—too far south if you let it. The bridges will be guarded. Going by ferry at the Water Gate will save you time. No one, not even the Border Lords, will cross there. They will go downstream, which takes a goodly day or so longer. It buys you time."

"Is the river dangerous?" He'd heard whispers, of course, but nothing concrete.

"Dangerous to those without a boat if they are, like the Border Lords, mostly human. Very dangerous for those of us who cannot cross running water."

"Except by bridge . . ." Aspen mused aloud.

"Except by a very high bridge," Jack conceded. "You should land in the Hunting Grounds at this time of year. You will have to travel on foot from there, over the Silver Hills and into Seelie lands. Be cautious, as the Borderlands may shift. If you find yourself there, be sure to travel only by day. Otherwise . . ."

Jack turned his back for modesty and Aspen quickly tugged on his leather traveling breeches and a fresh brown tunic before slipping his feet into his walking boots. "I hope my father's armies will be in the Borderlands by the time I get there."

"Yes," Jack said. "A hope. If not . . ."

Tunic on now, Aspen belted on his sword and tucked his dagger in his boot. He went back over to the chest and grabbed a shearling jacket for extra warmth. "I know my way through Seelie lands well enough, Jack, even though it has been years since last I was there."

He spoke with much more confidence than he felt. After all, he had been seven when sent to the Unseelie court. And though he had been out every day of his sixth and seventh year with either his father or his father's forester, learning the woods and how to live in them, how to cross the hills without hurt, that was seven long, lonely years ago.

When he turned back, Jack was sitting on the bed, the pack on his lap, as if guarding it.

Aspen swung the shearling jacket around his waist and tied the arms over his belly. Then he pulled the dark cape over his shoulders, pulling the hood up to disguise himself.

"I will not forget this kindness, Old Jack Daw," he said formally.

Jack nodded but didn't answer directly. "Be off now, Your Serenity. I've stuffed some things to eat into your pack— journeybread, some green apples, a small wheel of cheese."

Aspen nodded back. Best to be manly about it. No hugs. No tears. *No tears, no fears*, as his foster father liked to tell him, especially when in his cups.

There seemed nothing more to say, and Aspen knew he needed to hurry if he was to get to that boat before the guards were done being indisposed. He had no doubt that Jack had done the indisposing.

*Good man*, Aspen thought, and not for the first time. Though that wasn't right. Jack was a drow, neither fey nor finn, not quite creature and not quite a man. But certainly a friend in a place where Aspen had few.

*Well*, no *friends*, he thought bleakly, honestly.

"Thank you," he said to the air since Jack had somehow managed to leave before him. Without checking further to see where the old drow had gone, he rushed out of the bedroom door, pack on his back.

## 9

# SNAIL UNDERGROUND

*A*fterward, Snail realized she never should have opened the door without first looking thorough the keyhole. Looking might be dangerous, but opening the door turned out to be the true disaster. Though if she hadn't opened the door then, that would only have delayed the disaster, not averted it. She understood that at once.

The door screamed as it was opened. Or maybe that was Yarrow. Or one of the midwives. Snail was never to know.

The one standing there, hand raised to give the knock again, was neither the queen on her birth bed ready for their ministrations and competent hands, nor any of the four blind trolls who actually would have been much too busy holding on to the bedstead to knock.

Instead, at the door hulked a woodwose, his tangled locks all but obscuring green eyes, a snarling Red Cap holding tight to the cap that was ready to be dipped in their spilt blood, and three soldiers with a three-headed wolf straining at its leash.

"Oh!" Snail said in an unusually short and unusually quiet voice. She knew that the wolf could be tamed. She'd long ago learned several spells for taming wild animals, though she'd never actually used any of them. The woodwose and soldiers could surely be charmed. The midwives probably had such incants memorized. It was only the Red Cap, guided by a dark instinct, an unquenchable anger, and a passion for fresh blood, who was truly dangerous. The others were just there for show.

"Oh," Snail said again, this time in a whisper.

Behind her, making up for her reticence, the three midwives and Yarrow all began to wail uncontrollably, as if all small spells and incants had simultaneously left them.

Snail wondered if the birth tower was so warded that no spells other than midwifery magic could be done there. And the queen's magic, of course. Nowhere could be warded against that.

The women's wailing made the wolf lie down and whimper and caused the Red Cap to laugh. It was a strange cawing laugh, like the sound a murder of crows makes.

"It's her fault! Hers!" Yarrow screamed.

Snail did not have to turn around to know that Yarrow was pointing a finger like an arrow at her back.

But it didn't matter to the woodwose or the soldiers—or the wolf—whose fault it was, or if it had been only an awful set of circumstances. It was clear the guards had been sent by the furious queen to collect anyone left alive in the room. And collect them was what they planned to do.

What the Red Cap planned was anyone's guess.

The wolf, its ears still smarting from all the wailing, was of no use at all.

Actually, Snail felt sorry for the poor thing. Though she felt more sorry for the midwives and herself. She little cared what happened to Yarrow, but didn't say that.

Or say anything else for that matter.

❖ ❖ ❖

THE WOMEN WERE ALL bound together by silver manacles and led through a hidden passage down into the dungeon. Not iron, of course. No fey can bear the touch of iron. Being of a magical substance, silver worked well for binding but would not burn them to the bone.

Snail had never been in the passage and was surprised to see that it was opened by the tallest soldier lifting the torch out of a nearby sconce, and then yanking the sconce down with a swift pull. The mechanism made a groaning sound as if rarely used.

"All these years," Snail heard Mistress Yoke say, "and I never . . ."

A soldier growled at her, *"Haud yer wheesht, woman!"* And the wolf, now sufficiently recovered from the wailing, growled as well.

So Mistress Yoke shut up and didn't say another word. Nor did anyone else, though the Red Cap continued his cawing laughter long past the time there could be anything funny to laugh at.

The midwives, Yarrow, and Snail stumbled along down the stone steps. It was difficult to walk, chained as they were, and all the while the Red Cap poked at them with his bone knife, though not so hard as to let any blood actually flow.

Yet.

Snail wondered if he was just there to frighten them or was waiting to do them serious harm after.

*He certainly frightens me!* Snail was pretty sure he terrified them all, but she wasn't about to ask.

Yarrow limped, sniffled, and moaned, and each time it was her turn for a poke from the Red Cap's knife, she let out a little shriek as well. Each shriek occasioned another giggle from the Red Cap, which put everyone on edge. Even the wolf.

But Snail neither sniffled nor moaned. She observed. Or observed as much as could be seen between the torch's small light and the terrifying shadows on the wall.

And she counted, just in case it might be useful later.

They went down six flights of steps, which—Snail figured—included four flights from the tower to the ground floor, and then two flights belowground.

Suddenly, one of the guards gave the silver chain a hard yank. After that, Snail stopped thinking of anything but putting one foot safely in front of the other so as not to fall and drag them all down the stairs with her. But she didn't mind, for she'd already counted. It was a hundred and eighty stone steps—thirty steps between each floor—from the tower down to the dungeon, for it was clear that they'd come into the dungeon once they got to the final floor.

First there was the guards' station, which consisted of a table, two hard-backed chairs, and a stool, as well as an array of pikestaffs and broadswords lying against the farthest wall. On the table were pitchers of ale and three rather dirty-looking mugs.

*Or the dirt could just be shadows*, Snail thought, though she longed for a swallow, even of ale, which she never drank for it tasted bitter and gave her vertigo. But even ale would help, for her mouth had gone dry from the long trek down and the constant fear.

Strangely, there were no guards other than the ones who'd escorted them down the stairs.

Once past the guard station, Snail realized why. There were no other prisoners in the cells. Or at least no other *live* prisoners. But along the far wall were steel-barred cages with old skeletons—*skellies* Nettle called them—of people who'd died here, unhappy, unremembered, and unmourned.

*Well, maybe not unmourned*, Snail thought. They probably had families somewhere up above. But she doubted anyone would mourn *her* passing. Unless it was Mistress Softhands. And as Mistress Softhands was likely to die with her, maybe even *before* her . . .

At that, it was much too much, and Snail found herself shivering with terror. She thought she would cry then, but instead, she grabbed onto the anger she'd had earlier that day and added to it Yarrow shouting, "This is all *your* fault!" That turned her anger into a fury big enough to mount, and she rode it through the fear and came out the other side dry-eyed but still shaking.

*Sixty stairs*, she thought. *Sixty stairs between me and outside.*

Of all the things that might happen from here on out, this was all she knew for sure, and this was what she chose to concentrate on. She shut out the cackles of the Red Cap and the growls of the wolf and just kept thinking, *Sixty steps to the outside. And then I will be free.*

## ASPEN FOLLOWS THE WALL

*P*rince Aspen would have loved for the cover of darkness to be a boon to his escape. But in a court where half the nobles, servants, and livestock could see in the dark, not to mention the various hobs, goblins, trolls, the Wild Hunt, and the wolf pack, he—a Seelie lord—was the one at a disadvantage.

*I'd be better off sneaking away in broad daylight,* he thought. *The Unseelie are all a bit weaker during the day. Except, of course, for the Border Lords. And many will be sleeping.*

He positioned the pack a little more comfortably on his shoulders. *Nothing I can do about it. The time is not of my choosing. I have to go now. Otherwise they will come for me and sacrifice me and probably send my head to my father.* He bit his lip to keep from sobbing. Seelie or Unseelie, princes do not sob. *What was it my father used to say?*

He remembered then. It was the day he had been sent away. The whole court had turned out to see him off, crowding the palace courtyard. The noblemen bowed to him and mumbled useless clichés like "Keep your chin up, lad" and "You are a credit to your father."

Patting him on the head, the ladies of the court shed polite tears that their servants surreptitiously caught in crystal bottles for later use as spell ingredients. His mother, the queen, had done the same.

His brothers and sisters had wept loudly, looking at him with deep sympathy until he actually tried to meet their eyes. Then they looked away as if they were glad *they* weren't the ones going, and were ashamed of such thoughts. Even at seven he could read it in the way they turned from him.

Only Lisbet had hugged him, and stuffed something in his pocket when no one was looking. He had found it much later: a small silken packet in which she'd placed a locket with a tress of his mother's fine golden hair, a tiny glass jar filled with his favorite sweets, and a toy shaped like a unicorn that he had kept under his pillow as a little boy.

His father, the king, had walked with him to the outer gate and the great portcullis that now stood open. Beyond it, the Unseelie envoys waited, a pair of grey-faced drows with long noses and longer talons. Aspen thought they looked gruesome, despite being dressed in fine silk breeches and brocade vests. It wasn't till much later that Aspen realized that they were some of the more seemly creatures the Unseelie Court could have sent.

He reached for his father's hand to hold, but the king took his hand only to place it on the hilt of Aspen's small child's sword. A pinprick sword, his brothers called it.

The king neither wept nor mumbled.

"War does not call, it commands," he said. "Even kings and queens must do as it demands." He was quoting an old nursery rhyme.

Aspen looked way up at his father, who was standing tall and straight, his long white hair tucked behind pointed ears.

"And princes?" he asked.

The king nodded but didn't say anything more to Aspen. "Take him," he called to the Unseelie envoys. They came forward, bowing politely and with all deference, dressed in their black capes, and tunics, long dark trews covering their legs. The outline of the Unseelie Dragon was drawn in gold thread on the left side of each tunic. The two of them firmly gripped Aspen's arms. Their hands might have been made of oak, they were so unyielding. Perhaps they thought he might try to run away. Perhaps they feared he might faint. But he did neither, marching along with them as if he had been his oldest brother, Gann, doing his duty without once looking back.

The envoys took him directly to a waiting palanquin and parted the curtains. As he climbed in, the two drows leapt onto their horses, which were black as midnight, black—perhaps—as the envoys' hearts.

Aspen remembered being very proud of himself for not crying till the curtains had closed. The bearers—four ungainly-looking trolls, in shiny black trews and no other garb—picked up the palanquin as if it weighed nothing at all, and started off at a run after the horses, singing out a count as they went.

Only then did Aspen weep, where no one could see him. Unlike most seven-year-olds, he wept without sound, fat tears running down his cheeks and snot draining from his nose. When he finally stopped crying, he wiped his face on the curtain, and as he did so, he saw his family, his castle, his world disappear behind him.

❖ ❖ ❖

*War does not call, it commands,* Aspen thought, peeking down the hall to check for any late-night wanderers. He hadn't really understood the nursery rhyme then. *It doesn't matter whether I want to stay or go. War has made the choice for me. As it did for my father.*

Suddenly, Aspen was ashamed of how angry he'd been at his father earlier in the day. Now he realized that his father hadn't wanted to send him away. *That's what he'd been trying to tell me all those years ago.* Aspen frowned. *Of course, he could have just come out and told me that instead of always being the stoic elven monarch.*

Gritting his teeth, he thought, *If I ever have a child of my own, I shall speak directly to him.* Of course, if he didn't get away this day, he'd never have the chance.

The hallway in front of his door was clear and he walked quickly and quietly along.

*Eerie how silent the place is, how empty,* he thought.

Normally all the halls were abuzz with servants, underlings, cleaners, by day and by night. It was almost as if he were walking through an enchantment.

For a second he wondered what kind of enchantment it might be. Then he smiled wryly. What a silly thought! Of course—everyone was off preparing for the war.

*And of course, Jack will have made sure they have all been sent somewhere else.* His smile broadened, as did his relief. *Thanks, old friend.*

❖ ❖ ❖

WHERE THE HALL TEED, Aspen peered left, then right, appreciating the few guttering torches that still cast enough light for his weak Seelie eyes. There were few windows and the ones that existed were mere arrow slits. Unlike Seelie palaces that were built around courtyards that allowed the halls to be flooded with light, Unseelie castle interiors were purposefully kept dark, especially in the upper floors where the nobility lived.

*Well, I do have some choices,* he thought. *Like left or right?*

Having studied maps and mapmaking with Jack Daw, he knew the Water Gate was below Wester Tower, a small, guarded dock on a subterranean river that the Unseelie rarely used except in times of war or for secret messengers to come and go. Since the Unseelie folk were mostly uncomfortable around running water, they usually stuck to the ground roads. When forced to it, the dark forces were ferried across a river by the skeletal Sticksman, but few of the Unseelie could swim, except for the mer. And the mermen were untrustworthy allies, loyal to only themselves.

As he looked at the two halls leading from the tee, Aspen knew that either one would get him out of the central keep, but the left passage went past the Great Hall, which most likely would be full of gathering troops, while the right wound through isolated and sometimes totally unlit passages before exiting behind the Great Midden Heap.

Stinky and dark didn't appeal to Aspen very much, but he still turned right.

"War commands," he muttered. He couldn't afford to run into anyone. He would have a hard time explaining what he was doing in traveling clothes with a pack on his back. Most of the court knew he was a hostage, and the rest had surely heard the gossip. Better to risk the dark and the garbage.

❖ ❖ ❖

HE DIDN'T WALK LONG before the torches were no longer lit, though the last one he could see still sat in its sconce like a lever to an invisible machine. He thought about lighting it, but that would only be for comfort, and might attract attention he could not afford.

Chuckling to himself, though there was little to laugh about, he thought that he might even be better off navigating in the full dark. After all, it was the only way he knew that area.

Sun and Moon had once dared him to follow them down the unlit corridors, and he, of course, had followed willingly. They had quickly left him stranded, and he had spent nearly a whole day finding his way out—partly by trailing his right hand on the wall, and partly by following his nose. He had exited at the midden heap, vowing never to go that way again.

*But here I am.* He was well aware of the irony of the situation.

Trailing his hand once again on the wall, he kept his nostrils wide, trying to pick up the rotten stench that would signal the exit was near. The walls here were cold and damp to the touch; he remembered them from that long-ago trick played upon him. The walls would get colder and damper the closer he got to the Water Gate.

Keeping his footsteps light and his breathing soft, he listened carefully for anything that might be coming near.

*These unlit corridors,* he thought, *are about the last place in Faerie you want to run into anyone unexpectedly. Especially as a hostage prince.*

But when he finally did hear something, it wasn't the scurrying paws or scuttling footsteps he had been worried about. Nor the clang of steel hitting stone or the growl of a wolf or woodwose or troll.

It was something far worse. From what seemed like close by, but definitely muffled by a lot of stone, Aspen heard the sound of a girl screaming.

# SNAIL IN THE DUNGEON

*Y*arrow had already been screaming before they'd got down to the dungeon floor, though no one had even laid a finger on her.

Yet.

Despite the appalling noise, the soldiers had kept the group of women moving forward, the Red Cap giggling as if the sight of them struggling down the stairs was the funniest thing he'd ever witnessed, and perhaps it was.

*Or perhaps*, Snail thought, *he just has a brutal sense of humor.*

When they were marched past the skellies into the actual cell, she saw that the room was quite a bit smaller than the queen's birthing chamber with none of its amenities, just undecorated grey stone walls seeping moisture. *The birthing chamber*, she thought, suddenly aware that the queen and the baby had been far from her thoughts all this time. She wondered if it had been born already, whether it was a boy or a girl. *And who*, she thought, *had been in attendance?*

*And had anyone dropped the slippery child?* Then, as quickly, her mind turned back to her own dire situation.

As the women were unbound and pushed through the open door, the three-headed wolf lay down and began to moan. It had only two paws to cover its ears with, which left four ears open to Yarrow's screeching and the insane high giggles of the Red Cap. Clearly, the wolf was not happy.

In fact, the sound of Yarrow's screams was so unsettling, Snail wondered briefly if sticking a striped legging in the girl's mouth would help.

She hadn't gotten any further than that thought when someone put a hand on her shoulder, which made her jump.

When she turned slowly, fearing the worst, she saw it was just Mistress Softhands.

"Pretend she's in labor."

Snail nodded. Mistress Softhands was right, of course. If a woman screamed in labor, a midwife was trained to ignore the sound and stay on task. It was one of the very first things an apprentice learned.

*But what*, she thought, *is the task here?*

"Gag her," the captain of the soldiers said, pointing at Yarrow. The captain was a tall drow with one slumped shoulder and a scar on his face that pulled his lip down into a permanent sneer. His voice was dispassionate and firm.

One of the soldiers reached into his back pocket, pulled out a dirty nose rag with little bits of black snot still clinging to it, and headed toward Yarrow.

Yarrow's eyes had begun to roll so far back in her head, all Snail could see were the whites.

Without thinking it through, Snail rushed toward the soldier, palms up as if pleading.

"It's my fault," she said. "I'll calm her down."

But at that, Yarrow only screamed louder.

The soldier pushed roughly past Snail, grabbed Yarrow with one hand, and with the other somehow managed to stuff the tail of his rag into her mouth and then tie the rest around her head to anchor it. Yarrow was so cowed by the action, she didn't even try to tear the filthy thing away, only sank to her knees.

Horrified, Snail was nonetheless fascinated by the soldier's quick action and by the knot itself. She'd never seen one like it. *And best of all*, she thought, *it's worked!*

The dungeon room was suddenly and eerily quiet.

*Too quiet.*

Even the Red Cap was silent, having stopped his giggling to watch the soldier, though now he was leaning toward Yarrow as if waiting to see if she was going to suffocate or live, and clearly he was hoping for suffocation.

"That's better," said the captain. "Now, all of you women—listen carefully. Your lives depend on it." The scar on his face wriggled like a crawling worm as he spoke.

They listened.

*It's hard not to listen,* Snail thought, *with that incentive.*

The captain explained, almost if it pained him to say so,

that he would take each of them out separately for questioning by the Master of the Dungeon, an ogre named Geck.

"And when Master Geck is satisfied with your answers, and only then, you will be let go." When he finished speaking, the scar worm was still.

Of course *everyone* knew what happened to people whose answers an ogre didn't like. And it wouldn't be pretty, it wouldn't be painless, and it wouldn't be fast.

Mistress Treetop went with the captain first. Not her choice, of course. His. He kept his hand on her shoulder. He did it for control but she seemed to take it as comfort.

The other soldiers stayed to watch them, but from outside the cell, as if by separating themselves from their prisoners, they also separated themselves from their prisoners' fates.

❖  ❖  ❖

AFTERWARD, SNAIL UNDERSTOOD—though at the time she'd thought it very odd—that the women were questioned in a room close enough to the cell so their sobs could be heard as if the cell door had been left open, though not really close enough to understand what they were saying.

It was another way to keep them all frightened and atremble, and it worked, too. Snail tried to hold on to her anger, but the fear kept creeping through, and she worried that if she let it set up camp in her brain she would start crying and never stop.

*And then I, too, will be munching on a soldier's dirty snot rag.*

After each questioning session was done, Master Geck would rumble out to the captain to come and get the one questioned, take her back to the cell, and bring the next. This all of the midwives and apprentices could hear and understand full well, and it added to their fears.

Mistress Yoke and Mistress Softhands went out in turn after Mistress Treetop. All were still disheveled from the tumble they'd taken in the birthing room, and a bit lame from the forced march down the stone stairs to the dungeon. But when they returned, they each looked . . .

*Well, wrung out like pieces of laundry before the laundress has touched the cloth with the hot iron,* was Snail's first thought. Each came back with unkempt hair as if someone had tried to pull it out by the roots strand by strand. Their eyes were bright red with weeping. And the usually fastidious trio wore large blotches of sweat like dark wounds under the arms of their no-longer-well-starched dresses.

In addition, Mistress Treetop's hands wrangled together. Mistress Yoke twined her fingers through her hair nervously. And Mistress Softhands' eyes darted around the room, as if expecting something ghastly to leap upon her from every corner.

The questioning of the three women had not taken long, for none of them was trained in resistance.

And now the captain looked at the two girls.

First his gaze narrowed on Yarrow, though she was conveniently passed out, lying on the stone floor like a broken puppet with its strings cut, her swollen foot to one side. Mistress Yoke had taken a moment from her hand-wrangling to remove the gag from Yarrow's mouth, but it hadn't brought her around.

The captain turned his hard gaze next on Snail.

"You. Girl," he said in his commanding voice, the worm scar on the move again. Then he crooked his pointer finger at her.

Snail felt her knees weaken. She stiffened and locked them so as not to fall. When she felt her hands ball into fists, she willed them to open again, one stiff finger at a time. Something sour spurted up from her stomach into her mouth. She didn't spit it out, but swallowed it down instead. It burned hot and hurt coming up and going down, but not as much as she would be hurt if she hadn't the right answers for Master Geck, of that she was sure.

Realistically, she knew she had no choice but to go with the captain. But she glared at him as she went.

*Better angry than afraid,* she thought.

The glare didn't seem to affect him at all. In fact, he seemed somewhat amused by it.

❖ ❖ ❖

THEY WALKED SLOWLY down the hall. Actually, Snail would rather have walked quickly. *Get in. Get it over with. Get out.* Whatever *it* was. She refused to think ahead because that meant thinking about the ogre, his teeth, his bad breath, his nonsatisfaction with her answers. She couldn't think about her answers at all. She didn't know what the questions would be.

Instead she looked down and counted how many steps she took to get where they were going.

Thirty-seven.

That was all.

Thirty-seven steps.

Not even as many steps as she had from her bedchamber to Mistress Softhands's, which was forty-two, counting bed-to-bed as she often had as a child waking from an awful dream.

*Thirty-seven steps.* Then she thought, *And still only sixty steps to outside.* But thinking that no longer helped.

They turned to the right and faced a dark oaken door with a wooden latch.

"After you," the captain said. They were the first words he'd spoken since they'd left the dungeon room. He opened the door and stepped aside for her.

She knew this was not from politeness. It was to make sure she had no way to escape.

So she walked in head up, shoulders squared, through the open door, trying to keep herself calm. But at that very moment, as if it had been planned, Yarrow began screaming again, her voice bouncing off the stone walls.

And to make it worse, all three of the wolf's heads began howling.

The door slammed behind Snail but didn't cut off the

sound. If anything—a trick of the dungeon layout or magic or both—the sound was doubled. Suddenly she had no courage left in her. She turned to ask the captain to stay, but he'd already left.

She could hear him calling out to the others, "That cursed girl won't be stopping her bloody noise any time soon. Best we eat now back at the guard station where it's quieter. My men, you can start on the ale, and you—Red Cap—scramble up those stairs and get us some bread and cheese. Oh, and bring the wolf three bones."

And then with a scuffling sound, they were all gone past the dungeon master's cell, most of the torches with them. Except for a small candle in a sconce near the cell door, she was now in the pitch black. She'd never had good Unseelie eyes to see in the deepest dark and wondered if they knew that and had withdrawn the light to make her even more frightened.

Someone—something—huge in the small dark room she'd just entered, cleared its throat. Or maybe it growled. She couldn't tell the difference. But her heart sank all the same.

## ASPEN FALLS

*T*he girl's screams tweaked Aspen's princely instincts—his *Seelie* instincts—and he took two steps toward the sound before stopping abruptly.

"What am I doing?" he asked the darkness. He received no answer. "I have to escape, not rescue damsels in distress. If she is screaming that way, there is more than one tormentor involved. And *I* am out of time!" Those were *Unseelie* thoughts, but he didn't acknowledge that aloud.

*Besides,* he thought, picturing all the horrid creatures that made up most of the Unseelie Court, *the screamer is unlikely to be a damsel. It could be a banshee or a wolf girl or a morrigan or . . .* He turned away from the screams and headed back toward what he hoped was the midden pile and freedom.

The screams faded and finally stopped. He tried not to think about whether he was just too far away to hear them anymore or whether they'd stopped because the girl—*creature!* he told himself—could no longer draw breath. He tried not to think of himself as a coward.

"I could not help her," he muttered, then corrected himself again. "I could not help *it*. Whatever it was."

The stench of the midden pile was strong now, and the rock wall he dragged his hand over was rougher with occasional patches of moss. All signs that the corridor had turned to tunnel and the exit was near.

"At last."

The flight from his room, the long trek in the dark, the screaming creature—he was afraid that, all together, they had finally fractured his nerves. He needed to get outside in the fresh air and pull himself together. *Even if the fresh air holds the stink of the midden.*

He still had a long night ahead, and he had to find the Water Gate before whatever Old Jack Daw had done to "indispose" the guards wore off and he was then left with no means of escape. Stopping for a moment, he pulled a handkerchief from his sleeve to cover his nose—the smell of the offal steaming in the nearby midden was suddenly enough to burn his nostrils. Briefly he wondered how the midden lads stood the smell, then shrugged because it was an unprincely thought. Besides, they were bred up to it, as he was bred up to . . .

His mouth twisted with the next thought. *As I was bred up to be a hostage.*

He was *not* making a good job of it.

From up ahead, between him and freedom, Aspen heard talking.

"I hates the ones that screams likes that." The voice hissed and sputtered like a wet torch.

Aspen stuffed the handkerchief back in his sleeve and looked around desperately for another route to the outside. It was a remarkably futile gesture, for the passage remained pitch-dark and he still couldn't see a thing.

"But they all scream when Master Geck puts the questions to 'em," a low reply growled.

"And I hates them all," the first replied, not distinguishing whether he meant the screams or the dungeon master or someone else.

Aspen tried to back quietly away, but when he heard the voices again they were closer. *Much* closer. If the voices belonged to trolls or drows or woodwose, they'd smell him out in another few steps, even with the stench of the midden up their noses. Trolls and drows and woodwose, who made up most of the castle guard, were scent hunters. If he'd been worried before, he was terrified now and thought he could hear his heart thudding madly, nearly bursting through his tunic. He wondered if they could hear that, too.

He tried to think of a bluff, something to say to them, something to silence them with the Princely Voice, full of authority and snark. Usually, the underfolk could be cowed that way. But he doubted if anything but a squeak would come out of his mouth now, and they'd be on to him—and *on* him—in an instant.

*Think, Aspen, think!* he warned himself, but he was beyond thinking.

"It's not their fault they screams," said the growler. "Master Geck hurts them sumthin' awful."

"I don't *blames* them. I *hates* them."

*I have to get away!* Aspen thought. *But quietly.*

For a moment, he felt proud for having a reasonable thought in such circumstances. But putting that thought into action was proving difficult. He turned to sneak away and in the darkness didn't realize how close he was to the wall. The tip of his sheathed sword scraped against the stone. It wasn't terribly loud. Just the soft swoosh of leather against stone. But it was loud enough.

"What's 'at?" the hissy voice asked.

"Halloo?" growled the low voice, sounding a bit like leather against stone itself. "Halloo?"

Aspen froze.

"Halloo?" the low voice called a third time.

The hissing voice had gone quiet.

*Suspiciously quiet,* Aspen thought.

Then he heard a sniff, as if the guard, whatever creature it was, had gotten his scent, and after came the sound of the lightest of footsteps closing in from behind.

Aspen ran, taking off liked a scared rabbit running from a wolf, racing back into the sightless dark. He tried to keep his hand on the wall, but it was hard to do while running, and painful, too. It felt as if he left a pound of skin on the corridor stone every time he reached out to try to stay oriented. With every charging step, he feared he'd crash into a wall or trip over an unseen obstacle, and he knew he would surely be overtaken by whatever horrific creature the hissing, sniffing hater was.

*They will probably take me to Master Geck for questioning.* He caught his breath. When he breathed again, it was painful. *And I will probably scream, too.*

Despite the short length of the conversation he'd overheard, Aspen now knew quite enough about Master Geck to realize he didn't want to be questioned by him, and so he forced himself to run faster.

Suddenly, there was another scream.

*More of a yell, this time,* he thought, *and definitely a different voice.*

Thinking about the scream rather than his running made his feet tangle up on their own, and he fell.

"There!" he heard hissed from not nearly far enough away. "We has him!"

Aspen felt a little woozy as he came to his feet. *I wonder if I have hit my head.* There was no time to worry about it, though. He had to keep going.

Reaching out for the wall to help himself stand, he felt something protruding outward and knew it at once.

*A torch!*

He pulled it from its sconce with the vague idea that light

might help—if not to hide, then at least to keep him from falling again. And the torch could always become a weapon. Most Unseelie folk hated fire, just as they hated water. Perhaps he could keep the two hunters at bay with the torch fire long enough to kill them with his sword.

*And maybe I will grow wings and fly out of here.*

He knew that was a ridiculous thought: the royal Fey hadn't had wings for thousands of years.

*But I don't need wings to light a torch!* It was a simple matter for a full-blooded prince of Faerie to light a torch. So simple that it didn't even require words. Aspen took a deep breath, formed a single fiery thought, and focused on the torch, and it burst into brilliant flame.

Which presented a new problem. Because no amount of magic could prepare his eyes for the sudden bright light after being so long in blackness. If the creatures were blinded, he was, too, as blind in the light as he'd been in the dark.

And now he was dizzy as well.

*Definitely hit my head when I fell.*

He reached for the torch's empty sconce to steady himself. But instead of finding a firm handle to hold onto in the now-spinning corridor, he felt the sconce suddenly give way beneath his grip, almost like a lever.

Aspen staggered in surprise. There was a sound of stone grinding on stone and then a puff of wind that blew the torch out.

His next thought was: *Exactly like a lever*—as he plunged

into darkness and a wall that was no longer there. He couldn't tell which way he was facing or even which way was up, and when he took another step, his foot, too, met nothing but air.

For a moment he hung there by one arm over the black pit and heard the two sniffers laughing, as the hissy one said, "That goes straight down to the dungeon, that does. Let's head down there and watch the fun."

For a second he could make out their outlines—hairy things about his size, looking like weasels, with long pointy noses.

The bigger one kicked out and connected with Aspen's stomach, and the surprise of it made him let go of the lever.

*Boggarts!* he thought, and then—with nothing to hold on to and nowhere to stand, he tumbled away into darkness. But at least he didn't scream.

## SNAIL SPEAKS TO THE OGRE

*M*istress Softhands had often said, *When speaking to ogres make your sentences small and direct. Say things plainly. They are not subtle creatures.*

She'd neglected to say that in a darkened dungeon room, surrounded by damp walls coated with a kind of phosphorescent fungus that turned everything a vomit green, ogres smelled like death.

Snail tried not to sniff aloud, tried not to weep, tried not to fall to her knees in fear. She managed two out of the three. However, tears coursed down her cheeks unchecked.

"Girl," came the rumbling voice, "I don't want to hurt you."

Somehow, she didn't believe him.

Somehow, she refrained from saying that. She refrained from saying anything at all. She didn't want a trembling voice to give her away.

But she held on to what Mistress Softhands had said. If ogres were not subtle, then perhaps he *was* speaking the truth.

Perhaps. Seven letters that spelled out the possibility of life.

"But," rumbled the voice, "I do have some questions."

*And I have lots myself,* she thought. She didn't say that aloud, either.

In the dungeon's dark, she couldn't see him. Not really. Though she had a vague sense of something big and hulking moving in the shadows. The only light was a thin sliver of moon from a very high and very tiny window, which shone down on a plain wooden stool. Snail wondered if she'd be asked to sit.

"I understand, Master Geck," Snail said finally, her voice a shadow in the dark room. That it hadn't trembled was a miracle. The Unseelie didn't believe in miracles, though of course *everyone* believed in magic.

"I don't need understanding," the voice rumbled on, sounding a bit testy.

Snail didn't like testy. She wanted the low rumbling back.

"What *do* you need, Master Geck?" she asked as politely as she could. This time her voice shook. But only a little.

"Answers."

"I have answers," she said. "I have lots of answers. Any kind of answers you want."

"I want the *right* answers." Rumble. Grumble.

*This isn't going well*, Snail thought, *and we haven't even really begun.*

But evidently they had.

There was a shift in the air, and suddenly something grey, like a sliver of moon with fangs, smiled above her.

*It has to be the ogre grinning*, she thought, since it was just a little below the actual sliver of moon shining behind the bars of the single cell window. She couldn't begin to imagine why his smile should shine so. Surely an ogre wasn't interested enough in personal grooming to brush his teeth. *Or perhaps he brushes them with luminescent moss.* She wondered what he used for a brush. A twig? A carved stick? A finger bone?

She shuddered.

"Are you frightened, girl?" the rumble asked.

She realized that in fact she'd been thinking about brushing teeth and not about being eaten, an improvement of sorts, though both led in the same direction.

"I'm considering right answers, Master Geck," she said.

It was a kind of lie and somehow he knew. The grey smile loomed lower, broader, not at all jolly.

"Speak true," the mouth warned.

"I was thinking about tooth brushings," she said.

He began to laugh, and it was as if two people were laughing at her, one higher, one lower.

*Fascinating*, Snail thought, for a moment forgetting to be afraid. But she remembered again quickly when the ogre abruptly stopped laughing.

And a second later the other voice, the sort-of echo, stopped laughing as well.

"Tell me," Master Geck said, the grey grin and clean fangs appearing suddenly inches from her face. "Why did you try to kill the queen?"

"I didn't . . ." She tried to look the ogre in the eye, but he was gone now, stepped back into the darkness. "She isn't . . . ?"

Before she could finish her thought, there was a hot breath on the back of her neck and a rumbling in her ear that made her jump in shock.

*How does something so big move so fast? And so quietly?*

"Then whose idea was it?"

Turning to face the ogre, Snail said, "Wait. It wasn't anybody's *idea* . . ." but he was gone again.

"Best tell me soon, girl." From behind her, once more. Snail spun again, knowing it was futile, and was rewarded with a dark empty space and a low voice in her ear. "I don't want to hurt you."

This time Snail didn't stop herself from speaking. "I don't believe you."

Master Geck loomed up in front of her, close enough now so that he was outlined in the single candle's light, and even in the darkened room—the sliver of moon gave no light— she could finally see all of him. Even for an ogre, he was big. He was shirtless, his flesh a deathly grey green. Though he was grossly fat in the belly, his arms and legs bulged with impressive muscles. Lank hair hung over his giant ears and protruding brow, obscuring his eyes, perhaps to hide how surprisingly small and beady they were. He wore only a leather kilt held up by a straining belt from which hung no less than ten knives of various sizes. None of those sizes was small.

She shuddered. Those were not knives for mumblety-peg or sharpening a quill. They were skinning and boning knives. Those knives belonged to a butcher.

"But," the ogre said, bending over so that his face was directly in front of Snail's. He smiled widely and she could see that the rest of his teeth were as clean as his two long fangs. "I am getting awfully hungry."

As if to emphasize his point, he reached out a hand, and with a pointy black nail poked Snail hard in the stomach.

She supposed he meant the poke to send more shivers down her spine but it didn't. She hated being poked anywhere, and especially in the stomach. It didn't make her afraid. It just made her furious.

"IF YOU MEAN TO EAT ME," she shouted, "DO IT! JUST DON'T POKE!"

Master Geck looked taken aback, as if thinking, *Here is a wee speck of a girl who should be shaking in terror and is instead shouting furiously at me.*

*Ha!* thought Snail. *He doesn't like surprises.* She wondered if that was what Mistress Softhands meant about being unsubtle.

But the ogre looked even more taken aback when, with a groaning scrape and a few thumps and bangs, a back door to the room suddenly opened, and the prince Snail had

spilled drinks on just that morning rolled across the floor
to fetch up against their feet, a sputtering torch in his hand
and a pack on his back. He didn't seem to notice the giant
ogre. Instead, he gazed dazedly up at Snail.

"You!" he said, sounding more confused than angry.

"Who?" Master Geck said, sounding only confused.

That's when the prince looked behind him and, noticing
the ogre for the first time, gulped.

"Are you?" the prince said, as if completing the ogre's question. Standing quickly, he held the torch aloft. "Who . . .
Are . . . You?"

Snail thought he was trying to use the Princely Voice,
the voice that was used to make servants move faster. But it
squeaked a little too much to impress her, let alone the ogre.

The prince and the ogre began circling each other, shouting "Who?" and "Who" back and forth like a couple of
demented owls, almost as if they were playing catch-'em
with words instead of the usual chaff-stuffed balls.

None of it made any sense to Snail. She was much more
angry than scared now, and she didn't care how or why the
prince was here, only grateful—in a furious sort of way—
for the escape, even if it was only momentary. She certainly
didn't want to get eaten or beaten or otherwise abused. The
only thing that mattered, she decided, was that for the first
time since she came into the room, the ogre's attention was
elsewhere.

Grabbing the stool with both hands, she reached up as

high as she could and slammed Master Geck in the back of his head, where his neck and shoulders met. The force of it ran down both her arms. She hoped it would fell him.

The stool shattered and Snail felt a sting as a splinter from the broken stool jabbed her palm.

The ogre grunted in pain, staggered, but didn't fall. When he turned to face Snail, one hand on the back of his neck, he squinted down at her, his piggy eyes half shut. She hoped it was from pain.

Then he laughed. "Now I am going to eat you for certain."

She believed him, and—in her terror—glared.

The ogre took one step toward her and his piggy eyes suddenly glazed over, like one of Master Bonetooth's finest *fygeye* confections. Then, he spun around, grunted "Why?" turned completely grey, and fell forward, a mountain crumbling.

Snail stared at the ogre's lower back, at the knife jammed in it, as if it had grown there on its own.

*The princeling must be a lot tougher than he looks,* she thought. *And faster, too.* She hadn't even seen him move behind the dungeon master in all their circling.

"Thank you, sir," she said to the princeling, but he seemed dazed.

"For what?" he asked.

"For that," she said pointing to the downed ogre.

"Oh, Puck!" he said.

Seemed an odd reaction to his kill, but Snail didn't have

time to think about it. She reached for the knife and yanked it out with two hands. It was an elegant thing, looking much too thin and much too pretty to kill something as big and ugly as Master Geck. She dropped it, point first into her apron pocket, then grabbed the prince's hand and pulled him toward the now-gaping back door of the cell through which he'd so recently fallen.

"I'm getting out of here," she said, before suddenly remembering her manners, and adding, "Your Serenity. And I apologize for touching you. But I suggest you come with me."

"Oh, Puck!" he said again, wiping his hand on a silk handkerchief that seemed to have been stuffed up a sleeve. But he followed her as she stepped around the fallen ogre. The prince's still-guttering torch illuminated the door he'd just fallen through.

As if suddenly awakening, the prince said, "We cannot go that way. There are . . . creatures up there waiting. We need to go that way." He gestured toward the front of the cell.

"No getting out that way," she told him, working hard to keep her voice low and sensible when really she just wanted to scream like Yarrow. "Too many guards." *And cells and skellies,* she thought, but didn't say that, not knowing what princes were sensitive about—except about being touched. And splattered. "We're going up your new stairs."

"No!" he said, using the Princely Voice again, that hard,

low command that all royalty was born with. It didn't squeak this time.

*I guess it's easier to use the Prince Voice on an unarmed midwife's apprentice than on a giant ogre with a belt full of knives.* Then she remembered the knife she'd popped into her apron. *Well, not unarmed anymore, I suppose, but certainly not an ogre.*

"No!" the prince said again, using the Voice.

As a lowly apprentice, she had no way of disagreeing further, and simply followed him to the cell door. Since it was only locked, not bespelled, he opened it with a single wave of his hand and went through.

*I wish an apprentice's life was that easy*, she thought, going after him. *Or an escape.*

## ASPEN SPIES SKELLIES AND CELLS

*I cannot believe she touched me,* Aspen thought. *The cheek of the girl!*

Back home her kind were not even allowed to be regular house servants. They were the lowest of the low, fit for only the tannery or the mill or any of a dozen other filthy jobs that Aspen had but a vague knowledge of.

*Of course it seems I am in dire need of allies at the moment. So needs must. Even if her people are . . .* He shuddered and stopped himself. *She seems capable enough. She might be useful, if only as a hostage, something to trade if I have to.* He held back a giggle: *A hostage for the Hostage Prince!*

He thought of her whipping her knife out of the ogre's back and popping it into her apron pocket, pretty as you please.

*Where did she have it hidden? Surely they searched her apron before putting her in a cell. And how did she get it out and stab the ogre so quickly? And why did she first hit him with the stool?*

He shook his head. So many questions and no time to

answer them. The only thing he was certain of: she was not going to lead him. Especially not up the stairs he had bounced down. That led directly into the arms of the two boggarts. He was the prince; he *had* to be the leader.

"This way," he said, petulantly turning left—the no-exit way, according to the girl. But if she had not been that way before, how could she know?

"But," she said, "there's no door out that end."

"Follow!" he hissed. She had been obeying his kind her whole life and did so now, quick-stepping after him. But he could feel her glare between his shoulder blades.

For some reason, it made him smile.

His torch finally guttered out, leaving them in a gloomy hall. Only a single flickering candle lit the narrow hallway as they walked three dozen paces past rows of cells occupied by only the skeletons of long-dead prisoners. Probably left there to intimidate the weak-minded underclasses. He refused to let them intimidate him. Much.

"Oh!" the girl behind him suddenly cried. "Thank you, Your Serenity!"

Then she charged past him muttering something, and rattled the door of a cell that was actually inhabited by live prisoners.

"Mistress Softhands!" she called.

Aspen peered through the gloom into the cell. Three squat old midwives—as alike as toads—as well as one sylph-like assistant, who would be pretty if someone gave her a bath, all clambered to the bars squawking and squeaking at once. The only word Aspen understood was when the girl said, "Quiet!" in the same tone he had used on her just moments before.

*She is certainly a quick study*, he thought, almost in admiration. *But simply saying the word in that tone does not make her a princess. She was born without magic and with an ability only to serve.*

Still the women quieted—a little.

But when they spotted him, they began gasping, curtsying, and saying, "Your Serenity!" all at the same time.

It wasn't an improvement. And it was much too loud. *They will have the guards back in a minute*, he thought, *and that will not do any of us any good.*

"Come," he said to the girl. "We do not have time for this." He looked again at the awkward mass of bowing servantry. "Whatever *this* is."

The girl whipped her head around to glare at him, then with a visible effort turned the glare into a friendly smile. It puffed her cheeks and thickened her face. Made her look less fey.

It wasn't an improvement either.

"But, Your Serenity, we have to free them," she said. "They're my friends."

The other girl—by her apron and striped hose, an apprentice as well—shot his girl a look that did not seem all that friendly to Aspen. *Not* my *girl*, he quickly reminded himself. He would have to find out her name. Knowing something's name made it the more biddable.

"No!" the caged girl shouted. "We're not going anywhere with *you*!" Folding her arms, she backed away from the cell door. "You're the reason we're in here. You're just trying to get us into more trouble."

Aspen was not sure how much more trouble they could get in. *Did they not see all the skeletons on the way in?* It was obvious that few folks ever left the dungeons alive.

Two of the midwives looked as if they agreed with the pretty apprentice, taking up positions next to her on the back wall, arms folded angrily across their ample chests.

"Mistress Softhands?" the knife girl said to the last midwife at the cell bars.

The old toad turned her wrinkled brown face up and looked at the girl with what Aspen assumed was a kindly expression. He could not really tell through the wrinkles and the gloom, nor with the miles of social strata between them.

Reaching through the bars, the midwife patted the girl on the cheek.

"Go, Snail," she said. "There's blood on your apron and yon former hostage prince carries a traveling pack."

"*Hostage* prince?" The girl turned and stared at him. Or glared. It was hard to distinguish in the little bit of hallway light.

The old midwife added, "I don't think leaving with you two will do much to improve my lot."

"It might?" the girl said, turning it into a question, as if even she didn't believe it.

The midwife didn't answer the question, but said, "Go," again, and then changed her cheek pat to a fairly sharp cuff on the girl's ear. "And quickly, too! Be a rabbit today, Snail!"

The girl backed away rubbing at her ear. "Yes, mistress," she said quietly.

*Well, that was a waste of time,* Aspen thought, before realizing he now had the girl's name. Snail. *She had best be faster than that!* He grabbed her by the wrist—far more suitable than *her* grabbing *him*—and dragged her down the increasingly dark hall. On the way, he had another thought. *Now she knows I'm the Hostage Prince. She could trade me as quickly as I could trade her.* Perhaps she was a dangerous person to travel with after all.

They didn't get far. As the girl had predicted, the hallway ended in a very short distance at a plain wall with a final sconce holding an unlit torch.

"See," she snarled. Then, remembering her station, she quickly changed it to, "I believe I informed you thusly, Your Serenity." And gave a bow that Aspen felt wasn't nearly deep enough.

He did not deign to answer her. Instead, he stomped over to the sconce and pulled the unlit torch out. Smirking haughtily at the girl, he pulled down on the now-empty sconce.

It didn't budge.

Frowning, he pulled it harder.

Nothing.

Turning to face the sconce completely, he dropped the unlit torch and pulled hard with both hands. When that didn't work, he tried shoving the sconce from side to side.

It shifted ever so slightly in the stones, but no secret passage appeared to lead them to freedom.

He looked down at the torch as if the fault lay with that piece of wood, hay, and pitch. Then he looked at the girl. She was staring at him almost with pity, which was much worse than the smile. And infinitely worse than the glare.

She opened her mouth to speak.

"I know," he interrupted, "you have informed me thusly." He pointed down the hall. "Back."

The midwives and their assistant looked at them strangely as they strode past a second time, but none dared to say anything to the prince, escaping hostage or no.

*I'm sure they will be* more *than happy to tell the next noble who stops by all about the two of us,* Aspen thought. An underling's freedom had been bought for far less. He realized, having both a knife and a sword, he could easily silence them all, but he would not buy his freedom that dearly. Not slaying three old women and two girls. That might be an Unseelie thing to do, but—he had no doubt of it now—he was still Seelie at the core.

During the three dozen paces back to the cell that held

the dead ogre and the stairs, Aspen thought about whether or not he should pass it by and try to go out the easier way, past the guard station.

*But there might be too many guards at the station and Puck knows how many soldiers at the top of the stairs,* he thought. They were just going to have to risk the two boggarts that had been stalking him down the halls. Maybe he could bluff his way by. Or maybe he and the girl could dispatch them with sword, dagger, and some noble magic. *She was mighty quick with her knife.*

Still, he was not hopeful. The two at the top of the secret stairs had been hunters, assassins. They would be expecting trouble. The ogre, for all his bulk, had been slow and unsuspecting. *And as everybody knows, they are not,* he reminded himself, *a subtle race.*

*And further,* he admitted to himself dismally, *I have not had* really *proper sword training since I was seven.* Certainly not enough to best trained soldiers in a small setting. He had spells, of course, but the dungeon was surely warded against all major spellcraft, and though the girl was gifted with that dagger, there were two creatures—not just one—waiting above.

But his worries about the two creatures were suddenly swept aside, swamping all that he knew, much like a mighty bore in a river overturning even the most balanced boat, for when they reached the ogre's interrogation cell, just outside the door, Aspen all but tripped over two bodies stretched out in the hall. Even in the small light thrown by the cell's candle, he could see that their throats had been savagely cut and they were still bleeding into the rough dungeon floor. It had been so quietly and efficiently done, he had heard nothing.

Grabbing the candle, he knelt down, and held the light close to the boggarts' faces, noted they were hairy, pointy-nosed, and very dead.

"Boggarts!" came a voice at his ear. "What are they doing down here? They surely weren't there when we came out." It was the girl, Snail.

He did not say it aloud, but he was certain they were the two assassins who had been after him. He smiled and everything inside of him seemed to let go. *Nothing to worry about anymore*, he thought.

Keeping his voice steady, he said, "Never mind them. We do not know them. They mean nothing. We will go in, circumvent the dead ogre, and head up the secret stairs."

Surprisingly, she interrupted him. "Circumvent? What's that mean?"

"It means," he said, "to go around."

"Then say *go around*," she muttered, adding a bit more loudly, "if it pleases Your Serenity."

He thought the addition of the politeness at the end hardly excused her tone in the beginning, but he also felt that they were running out of time.

*I will try to correct her behavior later.* Looking at the

boggart bodies, he couldn't help adding to himself, *If there is a later.* To Snail he said, "I know the way out from the top of the stairs." He used his strongest Princely Voice, as if going out that way had always been his intention. And it was true. Well at least it had been true before the assassins had arrived. And now it was true again. The rest—well, it was bluff. He knew it. The girl might know it, too. But since she was of the underclass, he was certain she would never say any such thought aloud. "So, are you ready to stop arguing and—"

"Who killed *them?*" Snail asked, interrupting again. "And why?" She looked up at him with a kind of childlike puzzlement, as if this were a maze she could not think her way through.

"Why should I care?"

"Because someone is quite the dab hand with quiet butchery," she said. "And we don't know which side he's on."

Aspen wanted to ignore her. She was only a midwife's apprentice, after all. But his hand holding the candle obviously felt differently, because it suddenly began trembling, sending bouncing shadows across the stone walls.

He realized that now they had a brand-new worry. *Who—indeed—had killed the assassins? And why?* The girl had put her finger on the open wound and had not flinched. On the other hand, he had closed his eyes and tried to ignore it.

*This,* he thought, *is possibly a worse worry than the others combined.*

"Let us get out of here and into the light," he said. *Surely I have been traipsing around in these dungeons long enough for dawn to be near.* "Everything looks better there." It was something his father used to say.

*And maybe*—he hoped—*it is true.* After all, nothing could look any worse. Of that he was now sure.

# SNAIL'S FIGHT

*Into the light*. That suddenly sounded like the best idea in the world.

Following the prince—because that was what her class was trained to do since birth—Snail thought about what she'd just witnessed. As the prince had checked out the two dead boggarts, she'd stared at them over his shoulder.

Their throats had been cut with something large and inelegant.

Something like the ogre's butcher knives, the ones he'd worn in the belt around his waist.

But when she and the prince had passed by the dead ogre, he was still lying on his stomach, which concealed the knives. And he was as still as the two creatures at the door. So she knew he couldn't have been faking. Ogres were not subtle creatures.

*There's someone else in this game,* she thought. *Someone who doesn't care about killing, which argues for a toff. Some-*

*one who is fast, thorough, and inelegant, which argues for a Border Lord. Someone who kills without using magic.* She bit her lower lip. *Which leaves only another creature, or an apprentice.* She sighed. *Apprentices don't kill.*

She thought a minute, then amended that: *Unless they are apprentice assassins.* Not that she'd ever met any apprentice assassins. Or met anyone who'd met any.

It was a puzzle.

Puzzles made her head spin.

A midwife's apprentice was taught how to anticipate problems in the birth chamber, not solve problems left by killers. *Anticipate, alleviate, and then await—the midwife's creed.* What an assassin's creed was, she didn't want to know. *Cut, kill, hack, and hew, slice your prey through and through? And then slip silently away?*

She forced herself to watch the prince's back and keep up with him step for step across the interrogation cell. By concentrating on that, she got her head to stop spinning at last, but it didn't solve the puzzle.

She *hated* puzzles.

While she climbed the secret stairs behind the prince, she stuffed her right hand into her apron pocket and wrapped her fingers around the handle of the knife she'd taken from the ogre's back. Elegant, with a carved handle, and an exceedingly sharp point that she hadn't dared touch, the knife was the only thing that made her feel even a little bit safe.

*So why hadn't the prince taken it? Or asked for it back?* She shook her head, reminding herself that if there were a third player in this game, then the knife was probably his. And he, rather than the prince, had done the ogre in. *I definitely don't want* him *to come to get his knife back.*

Snail was lost in thought as they reached the top of the stairs, and she failed to notice the prince coming to an abrupt stop. She slammed into him for the second time that day, and he dropped the candle. It fell spinning to the floor, making their shadows dance crazily along the stone walls as if there were suddenly dozens of strange creatures in the corridor.

"I'm so sorry, Your Serenity!" she whispered as she bent to pick up the candle. It must have been magically lit, because it was—*thanks be to Mab*—still burning. But when she stood up again, she saw that the shadows hadn't lied completely, and there *was* someone else in the hall: a tall, dark shadow looming up behind the prince, spreading shadowy arms to grab him.

And that *someone*, Snail thought, was most probably the one who killed the two assassins and possibly the ogre as well.

Before she could move or even think, the shadowy arms grabbed the prince. He tried to jerk away, but the arms held him fast by the shoulders. Even by candlelight, Snail could see that the prince's face had gone bone white. It was as if she could see the skull beneath. Whether it was terror or something else, she couldn't tell.

"Let him go!" she shouted.

She heard a low chuckle, and it was not from the prince, who was still struggling against his assailant.

*That laugh* . . . she'd heard it before. Only she couldn't think where. She took the knife out of her pocket and held it up in her left hand, the candle being in her right.

"Let . . . him . . . go," she said plainly, each word enunciated in case the shadow assailant was from the Seelie Court and didn't speak their language. "Let him go now. I have a knife . . ."

She held it up and was pleased that her hand didn't tremble at all.

"Unless you are left-handed," the voice behind the prince said—it was low, controlled, and rather amused—"I think I have the better of you."

"I *am* left-handed," she said, bluffing, "and my knife is very sharp."

The low laugh came again. "*Your* knife, is it? Not unless you are a drow."

Unexpectedly, the prince broke free, turned to face his assailant, and said, "Jack, what are you playing at?"

"You *know* him?" Snail was astonished.

The prince said over his shoulder, "He is my best friend." He hesitated as if he'd said too much, then turned back to the drow.

And now Snail could clearly see the drow's hand, which— if she'd noticed it earlier—would have identified him sooner, the four-fingered hand with sharp black fingernails that gave away his clan.

"Answer me, in Obs's name," the prince insisted. "What are you playing at?"

The drow moved into the light.

Still holding the knife out in front of her, Snail raised the candle so she could see both their faces at once.

The prince looked furious, color now flooding back into his face. He had his hand on the handle of his sword as if any minute he'd take the drow's head off.

As for the drow—this Jack—he was old. She knew that few drows reached old age. They were a quarrelsome crew— the young males fighting in the nest and eating their dead, and the adolescent males battling to the death over mates. That Jack was this old and a friend of the prince meant he was smart, lucky, and ruthless. She didn't like the sound of that combination.

"Ask him," she said to the prince. "Ask him again."

"Ask him . . . what?" the prince said, turning toward her, narrowing his eyes, almost hissing.

She realized at once that she might have just made a fatal mistake. The problem was she'd never had real occasion to learn proper manners. Birthing mothers don't care if the midwife addresses them correctly; they just want the babe out NOW! And the prince had seemed forgiving of her lapses in manners when they were alone and creatures were dying mysteriously all around them. But she knew that toffs could get really prickly about all that manners stuff when they were gathered in one place. Not that the drow was an *actual* toff. But still . . .

More than one head had been lost at court because of a dropped address or a misused title.

"Ask him again, Your Serenity, if it pleases you," she said, dropping quickly to one knee.

He turned back to the drow and said casually, so no one would think the girl had commanded him, "What *are* you playing at, Jack Daw?"

Not to be outdone, the drow bowed his head. "Just trying to keep you safe, Your Serenity." He winked one bright eye at Snail and stuck a dark nail into his mouth as if loosening a bit of something lodged in his teeth. When he withdrew the nail again, he added, "It looked like you were falling there."

The prince straightened his tunic. "I was fine. The girl bumped into me is all."

The drow peered at Snail as if his old eyes were having trouble piercing the darkness. She wasn't convinced.

"A midwife's apprentice? Interesting." He turned back to the prince. "Shall I keep her safe as well, Your Serenity?"

"Well . . . yes . . . I suppose . . ." the prince stammered, then caught himself. "Yes, of course," he said, sounding more regal, more commanding. "She has proven useful in my escape."

"Your escape seems to have needed many such useful folk already," said the drow. "And it is barely begun." He seemed to be controlling the urge to laugh.

"It is no laughing matter, Jack."

"Am I laughing, Serenity?"

Snail thought, *Close enough as to be no never mind*, which was something Mistress Softhands often said.

"Then let us get moving." The drow's voice was coolly in control. "The guards will find your two other useful friends at the bottom of the stairs before long." He turned and said to Snail in a tone that was both commanding and wheedling, "I suggest you put the knife away lest you fall against the prince again and injure him with it. It looks quite . . . lethal." Then he walked away from them, along the corridor.

Snail dropped the knife back into her pocket but kept hold of the candle with its flickering light, not wanting to miss any of the drow's movements. He may have wanted to help his friend. But she guessed he didn't *really* want to keep her safe at all. Or alive.

However, she knew he would do his dirty work in the dark where the prince couldn't see it. His kind always did. More reason to hold the candle high.

She was in this fight and flight alone, as she had been from the start.

*It's best not to forget that*, she told herself.

# ASPEN AT THE TOWER

*Th*ey exited the dark corridors and found themselves by the Great Midden Heap. It steamed into the morning, curlicues of stench and smoke intertwined. Nearby were long, thin patches of furrowed gardens with giant vegetables overflowing the rows.

*The smell,* Aspen thought, *is indescribable. And unbearable.* He glanced around. Except for the gardens, nothing grew on this land and it sloped away to the great, rushing river about a mile down hill from there. *Nowhere to hide on this open border,* he thought. *A very vulnerable spot.* He wondered if any of the Seelie weapons were trained on this place—the catapults and other siege engines that his father had been so proud of—the catapults especially, which could sling huge boulders across great expanses.

Squinting, he tried to look at the other side of the river, but it was too far away. Besides, the midden smoke was much too thick for him to see anything but the dark water with its occasional whitecaps of waves showing where rills and rocks lay.

Jack Daw made a hand signal at Snail, squeezing his thumb and pointer fingers together, and she nodded, showing that she understood he wanted her to extinguish the candle before they crossed the gardens. Aspen nodded, too, at how quickly she had caught Jack's meaning, immediately pinching the light out, so that its single smoke curl faded into the larger midden cloud.

Then, in single file, they followed after the drow, stepping over huge ungainly turnips and carrots and marrows that all looked more like enormous orange-colored sausages than the elegant vegetables served up at the king's table cut and molded into fanciful shapes like dragons and chimerae and other creatures of the Unseelie bestiary.

Though the vegetables were huge, they were only huge for vegetables, and provided no actual cover for Aspen or his two companions on their short journey from the midden heap to Wester Tower. He knew the tower by the description Jack Daw had given him, but he was glad to have the old drow lead them to it. Mistakes at this stage could cost him his life.

The tower was not all that tall aboveground, but it went a long way down *into* the ground. It was never a good idea for the Unseelie folk to march across great stretches of land in the daylight; their eyes were meant for darkness. So when they were forced to cross this expanse, they'd had captive Seelie slaves build the tower and its tunnel system. It had been a boon for their sorties into Seelie land. Jack had once told him that when the Border Lords had become a part of their armies, the Unseelie Court had finally an overground as well as an underground troop.

"Made us stronger," Jack had said, in that flat way he had of speaking. "Though getting them to follow orders is like herding sheep. It takes dogs and a good whip hand." Aspen remembered how the drow had laughed at his own witticism, a kind of harsh cawing.

Seeing the gardens—which must have been tended by day by Seelie slaves or changelings stolen from the human folk—as well as getting his first look at the mile-long run down to the water along open ground, Aspen only now really understood why the tower was so important.

*All the more reason to marvel at Jack's thoroughness,* he thought. *No guards anywhere.* He sent a good-health spell toward his old tutor's back and was pleased to see Jack's shoulders straighten a bit.

But a random thought ruined his good mood as they reached the tower and stared down into darkness.

*From one dungeon to another.*

Still, it didn't matter what lay below them. He knew the Water Gate was at the very bottom, and so down into the earth he would go.

❖ ❖ ❖

WITHOUT COMMENT, they started down the spiral stairs that wound widdershins into the earth.

The stairs were stone—dark, uneven—but Jack strode down them surefooted and swift. Aspen followed behind, trusting to his tutor's night vision. However, Snail trailed well behind, and for the third time in as many minutes, they heard her stumble and curse.

Aspen turned his head and whispered, "Snail, keep up!"

"Snail, is it?" Jack Daw said. "Aptly named."

"It seems so," Aspen agreed. He did not mention how swift she had been to kill the ogre and to take the knife from its back.

They walked down the stairs for what seemed like hours. *Or at least*, Aspen thought, *my knees seem to think it's been hours.*

Snail began to drop farther and farther behind.

Finally, they stopped to let her catch up a little.

"Are you sure we cannot leave her?" Jack Daw asked. It wasn't the first time.

*That is awfully tempting*, Aspen had to admit. The girl was annoying and only barely knew her place. But every time he thought about agreeing with Jack Daw and abandoning her on the dark staircase, he remembered how she had faced down the drow with her knife in one hand and the candle in the other, looking half-ridiculous and completely fierce when she said, "Let . . . him . . . go."

*Of course,* he thought, *that was before she found out that Jack was our friend.*

*Our* only *friend,* Aspen reminded himself.

He frowned at Jack and tried to copy one of the apprentice's glares. "No, we cannot. And do not ask again."

Aspen did not think his glare impressed the old drow, but Jack managed a bow and said, "As you wish, Your Serenity."

❖ ❖ ❖

SNAIL FINALLY CAUGHT UP. She was having a bit of trouble drawing breath, and her hair no longer stood straight up but was lying on her head in tendrils. *It makes her look more feminine,* Aspen thought. *Not beautiful like the twins, of course, or even pretty like the other apprentice in the dungeon. But more . . .* He tried to figure out what he meant and could only come up with *more presentable.*

However, Aspen noted, she was also neither limping nor shuffling, so at least *her* knees did not hurt.

"Shouldn't we be quieter?" she whispered.

Aspen was again annoyed that she didn't address him properly, but she had a fresh bruise on her cheek from her latest stumble, and perhaps she did not need to perform a curtsey when she was using the word *we.* He'd never been a *we* with a servant before, so he was unsure of that protocol.

It was Jack who answered, and sharply, putting the girl in her place. "There is no one near."

"I was thinking of assassins," she said.

Jack laughed and Snail looked startled, though whether it was because of his laugh or something else, Aspen could not guess.

"I think," Jack said slowly, curiously aware, like a wolf readying to pounce, "I think those were taken care of."

"I mean more assassins. Or guards. Or . . ." She ran out of options, or perhaps words.

Jack tapped his long nose with a black fingernail. "I'd smell them if they were about."

"How can you smell anything but the Great Midden Heap?" Aspen asked, voice rising in exasperation. The midden may have been well behind them now, but the stench still lingered in his nostrils.

Jack chuckled. "For all the hours of the night and day, I deal with kings and queens, and the courtiers who sniff at their heels, young Serenity."

"I fail to see your point." Aspen hated it when Jack did this—said something that seemed to make no sense, before offering an explanation, at which point it suddenly became painfully obvious that Aspen should have known the point all along. Aspen knew he was supposed to learn something whenever the old drow spoke that way, but it just made him feel stupid. And somehow everything seemed much worse now that Jack was showing him up in front of an apprentice midwife.

"I do not see how you can miss the meaning," Jack said,

quickly adding, "Serenity," as if that alone could take the sting out of what he was saying. "My point is that I am completely immune to the smell of rotting dung."

Aspen heard Snail stifle a laugh behind him. It made his face burn in the darkness. "Very droll," he managed.

"My apologies if I offended you, Your Serenity." Jack sniffed the air. "But do you know what I smell now?"

"What?"

"Water," Snail said.

"Water," the drow said as if Snail had never spoken.

As soon as the word was in the air, almost by magic, Aspen could smell the water. And hear it, too, a strong subterranean rumble of water pounding on stone.

"Water," he whispered. It was a promise, a prayer, and a deep sigh.

❖ ❖ ❖

THEY MANAGED TO get down the next ten steps at a run, Aspen in the lead, though he slowed to finish the final ten steps with a bit more care. He was glad to have done so, for the stairs ended abruptly in a huge cavern lit by long torches like spears magically thrust into the stone floor.

Looking up, Aspen could see neither ceiling nor stars, and was amazed by how far into the earth they'd come.

The ground was clear of upthrust rocks, having been carved away to make transfer of troops or treasure from the dock to the stairs easier. He had no idea how long it had taken, how many slaves had spent how many months down here at work. Probably under the whips of dwarves, who were the Unseelie Court's stone carvers. Huge chain-like rocks hung from the unseen ceiling, hinting at how big the upthrust rocks must once have been.

Hard-packed dirt marked a trail that pointed them to a small shack and a wooden dock at the far end of the cavern. They walked the trail carefully. Now was not the time to trip and break a limb, nor the time to make any unwanted noise.

Next to the shack stood a tall, incredibly thin creature in a long, black, hooded robe. Clearly the creature—*an it or a he?* Aspen could not tell—was the ferryman, for he was holding a poling staff nearly the height of the ramshackle building. He—it—could have been standing there for hours. Or even days. He—it—made no movement even now, or at least none that Aspen could see.

*A he,* Aspen finally decided, never having seen anything like the ferryman before. The creature reminded him of the kind of bugs that could camouflage themselves like sticks so completely, birds could not distinguish them from the twigs on which they sat.

Looking around carefully, Aspen saw there was no one else around. No soldiers, no guards, no assassins. Jack had indeed done his work well. Aspen was careful not to ask how he had disposed of the guards. He was afraid Jack would tell him.

Or—worse—show him.

The ferryman turned his buglike head toward them, and even from this far away, Aspen felt pinned by the stare of the pale, pupil-less eyes that filled most of the thing's face.

"What *is* that?" breathed Snail.

"The Sticksman," Jack Daw answered her, but looked down at Aspen. "He will ferry you over the river. I hope you brought coins."

## SNAIL TIES A KNOT

*A*spen started forward without waiting for the others, but Jack Daw put a hand on Snail's shoulder. She could feel his nails dig into the flesh, hard enough to hurt but not so hard as to bring blood. She marveled at his control even as she feared it.

"Not so fast, apprentice," he said, and laughed at the fearful look on her face.

*I've heard that sound before,* she thought, *and it wasn't that long ago!*

Only then did she finally realize who the old drow was— the other laugher in the ogre's room, watching and listening in the shadows as she had been questioned. Probably drinking in her fear and her anger as well. It was said drows loved to feast on famine and gnaw on the bones of the near dead. Said part in admiration and part in awe.

She wanted to ask him *why*, but didn't trust herself to say the right thing, so was silent, waiting to hear what he had to say. But she turned her head and glared at him. He made no return of her glare. Indeed, it was as if he hadn't even noticed.

When he spoke again, it was not what she expected to hear.

"You must tie me up," he said. "Tightly. As if making sure I could not stop you from getting into the boat. Then when I am found—and I *will* be found—I can tell them truthfully that the girl tied me up and the prince escaped. No Truth-seeker will be able to get any more out of me than that."

She knew there had to be more than this simple explanation. Yes, Truth-seekers could sniff out untruths. So what he said made sense—as far as it went. Still, he was leaving so much out. For starters, why he wasn't coming with them, how he knew he'd be found, what he'd been doing in the ogre's room. And now she realized he was the one who killed the ogre. He *had* said it was a drow's knife!

"But . . . but . . ." It was all she could manage.

"No buts. It must be done. Otherwise, the blame will fall entirely on my shoulders, and I could then no longer help the prince."

She nodded, as if she understood, but she didn't. She thought, *Once we are in the boat and across the water, why should it matter if Jack Daw can or can't help the prince? The prince—and I—will be beyond the drow's reach, and beyond the Unseelie king's as well.*

At least she hoped that much was true.

"What can I tie you with?" She realized she'd made up her mind to do the binding the moment she spoke. Jack

Daw's motives no longer mattered. She would be safer if he was unable to change his mind about helping the prince, because where the prince went, she went.

*At least until I'm in Seelie lands.*

The drow was already reaching into a deep pocket of his robe. As he pulled out a long braided rope—the kind the hangman used—she understood how planned out the whole escape had been.

*Though not*, she thought, *my part of it.* She had been an unwanted knot in the drow's escape rope from the beginning. Of that she was sure.

"How should I tie you?"

He laughed, that now-familiar sound. "You choose."

She figured he didn't expect her—a mere girl, an apprentice, an *underling*—to make a good job of it. But midwives had to learn to knot well. Yes, they worked with tiny sutures, but they tied them surely and with swift fingers.

*A knot*, she thought, *is a knot. I will tie you up tight, old drow. You will not get out of this bond as easily as you think.*

She took the rope.

Their eyes met. This time when she glared at him, he looked away. But a smile played around his severe mouth as if he knew something more and was not telling.

*Well, I know something more, too*, she thought. *I know you were in the room when the ogre was questioning me. And I know how to tie knots.* If she was lucky, at least some of that would give her an edge.

"Turn," Snail instructed him, her voice soft sounding but with a hard edge beneath. Quickly, she looked over at the prince. He was paying the two of them no mind, assuming—in his toffee-nosed way—that they were surely following. He'd almost reached the Sticksman and the flat-bottomed ferryboat. The boatman was facing them and saw what was happening between the apprentice and the drow, but he showed little interest, at least as far as Snail could tell.

"Hands behind you," she told the drow, in the same soft voice.

"Sir," Jack corrected.

"Hands behind you, *sir*," she said, then began to bind him tightly. He tried to move his wrists, seeking a more comfortable position, and she gave the rope another swift, hard twist, which stopped the movement, causing him to grunt out loud.

His shoulders hunched. She could feel the tension all the way down to his hands.

Then she took out the knife, cut a piece off the hem of her skirt, and, coming around to the drow's front, held up the cloth.

"I think silencing you is an even better idea," she said.

His yellow eyes got huge. There was a powerful fury in them. But he was not looking at the hand that held the cloth. He was looking at the other hand, the one that held the knife. He opened his mouth to yell something at her and she stuffed the rag in.

"There," she said, "you can tell *that* to the Truth-seeker as well. It may buy you a pardon and us more time, should we need it." Putting the knife back in her pocket, she bent down and searched his robe. She found two huge butcher knives with obsidian blades and put them into her own pocket.

"I don't think you will be needing these now." She smiled.

He growled something indistinguishable through the rag, but curses—as she well knew—didn't work through cloth. To be extra certain, she cut off another piece of her hem and wound it twice around his face to bind the mouth rag, then tied the ends securely at the back of his head.

"There," she said, "that should hold you until we are on the water. And Unseelie curses do not go any easier over the water than do Unseelie folk." She shuddered a moment, thinking about the water, hoping that unease on water was only true of the Unseelie lords and the creatures, and not the underlings like herself.

Then she turned and raced after the prince, who had just reached the ferryboat and was even now speaking to the Sticksman, who'd bent over nearly double to listen to what was being asked.

## ASPEN IN ROUGH WATERS

$\mathcal{U}$p close, Aspen decided, the Sticksman was even stranger to behold. His eyes weren't actually colorless, but the very lightest of blue, like a midwinter sky or an old robin's egg. And he smelled of something strange, something sweet and decayed: rotting pear or last feast day's pudding. Aspen felt as if he'd met the Sticksman before—though he was certain he hadn't—or that he would meet him again someday. It was a strange sort of feeling, and he had to physically shake it off, like a wet dog, before getting down to the business of the ferry.

"How much to cross the waters, riverman?" he asked, trying to sound more confident than he felt.

The Sticksman bent over strangely, his waist apparently where Aspen would have thought his chest should be. "Two pennies for each passenger and a silver for the Sticksman." He cast a blank gaze over Aspen's shoulder. "Four pennies and a piece, it seems."

"What?" Aspen said. "We are plainly three." He pointed

to Jack Daw and the girl. Or tried to. They were no longer behind him. Exasperated, he turned and followed the Sticksman's gaze to see Snail walking slowly toward them, while Jack unaccountably sat on the ground behind her.

"What in the three kingdoms . . ." he began, then stopped. He saw movement in the gloom by the cavern entrance. The movement quickly became figures. He was not sure from this distance, but there was really only one thing they *could* be with that height and brawn and chest armor, kilts below . . .

"Border Lords!" he shouted to Jack and Snail, hoping that conveyed the situation and its urgency.

Snail's head whipped up and she looked toward the entrance. She understood immediately and began running toward Aspen.

*Why is he still sitting there?* Aspen thought, then yelled again. "Jack!"

Jack didn't move, and now it was too late. The Lords had reached the old drow. Two stopped and swung their weapons at his back, but the rest came on. Aspen could see the shine on their armor and the drawn weapons, and knew he should be doing something, but he was transfixed by the sight of his only friend in Unseelie lands being slaughtered like a trussed ox.

*Mab take that stupid girl!*

Only Old Jack Daw wasn't dead. And not dying, either. In fact, he was lurching to his feet, his arms—which had been bound behind him—released by the Border Lords' swords. He was spitting something out of his mouth.

*What a plan!* Aspen thought admiringly. *He is keeping them occupied whilst we escape!*

Jack was now pointing at Aspen and Snail and shouted something Aspen couldn't make out because Snail had finally reached him and was tugging at his arm.

"Let's go!" she cried. "Now! Now!"

Her tone finally spurred him to action and he was right behind her when she leaped into the long, thin boat. An arrow whizzed past his head and he threw himself down, stretching flat on the bottom of the boat. His head was right next to the Sticksman's feet, the creature somehow already aboard though Aspen had never seen him move.

There was a dull *thunk* and the tip of an arrow was suddenly poking through the side of the boat.

"Time to go, Sticksman," Aspen called to the ferryman, who stood calmly at the back of the boat, his long pole in the water.

The Sticksman looked down and said placidly, "The coins, young master."

Three more arrows *thunk*ed into the boat and Aspen tried to make himself as skinny as possible. One arrowhead had landed right next to his eye, and he found himself momentarily admiring the workmanship of the thin stone tip.

Then sense returned and he screamed up at the Sticksman, "I am a prince of Faerie!" His face was hot with anger and fear. "When we reach my home my father shall shower you in coin!"

The Sticksman cocked his head to one side. "I do not require a shower of coin."

The arrows stopped and Aspen heard running footsteps on the dock. He felt tears prickling his eyes. *To come so far and be stopped now because of a greedy oarsman.*

"I require two pennies per passenger and a silver for the Sticksman," the Sticksman said, now addressing the runner.

"I have pennies," Snail cried as she scrambled on her knees to the Sticksman. She reached into her apron and produced four small copper coins. "Midwives always carry coins in case we lose both mother and child," she explained to Aspen, "and need to pay the Soul Man."

When Aspen looked dubious, she added, "To put on their eyes for their passage to the Land of the Dead."

"Land of the Dead?" he said witheringly, as one would to a child who still believed in Father All Fur delivering presents at the Solstice.

"And the silver?" the Sticksman asked, as he took one hand off the steering pole and pulled a long bone knife from his belt.

Aspen glanced at Snail, who shook her head. Then he looked back up into the Sticksman's big blank eyes, trying not to stare at the knife, trying not to tremble. "I carry no silver," he said at last.

"Your kind never does," the girl snapped. "And, of course, your friend didn't supply it."

"*He* had no time," Aspen snapped in return, emphasizing his own doubt.

But the Sticksman nodded. "Then you shall owe me a single favor."

Aspen's instant thought was that a favor from a Seelie prince was worth a lot more than one silver coin, though that thought seemed uncharitable given the situation. And, eyeing the knife, possibly fatal. But before he could agree, a young Border Lord leapt into the boat, bare knees flashing below his kilt.

"I have you," he cried, hand reaching for Aspen's throat and smiling so broadly his teeth looked like fangs.

Quick as a snake, and as deadly, the Sticksman lashed out with his dagger.

Without a single cry, the young Border Lord tumbled backward into the water, which suddenly boiled with a red foam.

"He did not pay," the Sticksman said, voice blunt as a cudgel. "No one boards without payment or promise."

Gulping, Aspen looked over the side of the boat at the red foam. His throat seemed ready to close, so he turned and said quickly, "A favor. Agreed."

The Sticksman pushed lightly on the pole and the boat sped away from the dock, faster than it should have, but not fast enough for Aspen's heart, which seemed to be beating in his throat.

*There's magic at work here, but none I recognize,* he thought. It was old magic, from before the time of the fey. He had heard about the day the Unseelie uncovered the cavern and found the Sticksman, who was already there, pole in hand. Aspen had thought it just a tale but now was no longer certain.

*Owing such a creature a favor,* he thought miserably, *is probably a bad bargain.*

Still, they *were* on the water and heading toward the other side.

*Whatever gets me home,* he thought. *And I am a prince. I will keep my promise.*

More arrows hit the boat. Even more arrows missed their target and fell in the water. Aspen could hear them splash.

The Sticksman didn't seem to notice, and no arrows came anywhere near him, as if he were, somehow, invulnerable to them. Or warded against them. "You will need to stand now," he said. "And draw your weapon." He looked pointedly at Aspen's sword.

Aspen chuckled, though with very little humor. "Not till we are out of bowshot."

The Sticksman didn't offer an argument. He just shrugged and said in his affectless voice, "They come."

There were more splashes than *thunks* now, and Aspen risked a quick peek over the side. Though only twenty pushes on the pole from the dock, the boat was moving swiftly away from the Unseelie shore and heading for the Hunting Grounds. The Border Lords were swarming on the sands, and five of them, one a red-bearded giant, were clustered at the end of the dock. But they could not go across, as there were no other boats or ferrymen. Still—so it seemed—Jack was pushing them into the water, pointing at the receding boat, shouting at the Border Lords to swim after, to shoot.

"Follow!" he screamed. "Or the king will have your heads. If he gets to the farther shore, this is war!"

*He is good*, Aspen thought. *No one will connect him with my escape and we are already out of reach.*

The Border Lords seemed oddly reluctant to go into the water, though they—unlike the faerie folk—could swim. Aspen had seen them ford shallow streams, and bathe in pools. But here only a few of the younger ones were venturing into the shallows, several in water up to the bottoms of their kilts. They shook their swords and staves in the boat's direction but did not try to go farther out.

Aspen ducked back down. "No they are not coming," he scoffed. "They cannot possibly swim to us. The river is swift and deep, and see—they are already backing away. They will have to go the long route. Jack has planned it all well, even to giving himself an alibi."

The Sticksman glanced over Aspen's shoulder as the arrows began falling again. "Not *them*," he said witheringly before nodding toward the front of the boat. "*Them*."

Aspen followed the Sticksman's gaze, but could see nothing except the boat's high prow where Snail lay, clutching three knives. He recognized one she'd taken from the ogre's back. The other two he did not remember seeing at all.

Suddenly, with a roar, a big green wave smashed into the bow and sluiced down the shallow deck, sending Snail sliding along with it. She slammed into Aspen, nearly impaling him with the smaller knife.

He fell backward into the Sticksman's legs, which felt thin, bony, and fleshless beneath the robes. The roar of rushing water went on, as if they were now in rapids Aspen had not noticed before, but the high waves hitting the boat had calmed.

"There is blood in the water," the Sticksman intoned.

"Yes, well, you put it there," Aspen said. *Rather snippishly,* he thought. Though given the situation, he could forgive himself the tone. He might have said more, but he was trying to disentangle himself from Snail. Unfortunately, she was trying to stand at the same time, and he ended up tripping her instead.

She fell hard into his stomach and he felt the air leave him in a rush. He struggled to push her away.

"Oh, be still!" she shouted.

*Mind your station!* he thought angrily, but did not have his breath back enough to say it.

"And as I hold the steering pole," the Sticksman said, "so it holds me."

"What does *that* mean?" Aspen managed to croak.

"It means he can't fight," Snail said.

Over the roaring water, Aspen heard a new sound. An eerie hooting, long and low, like the bottom note on one of Moon's bone flutes.

"Fight what?" He finally had breath again.

"Them," the Sticksman said.

The hooting stopped, and the arrows as well, and in the relative silence, Aspen suddenly heard the shouts from shore turn to shrieks of surprise.

And pain.

"The mer," the Sticksman added, a bit too eagerly.

*And*, Aspen thought, *with a bit too much satisfaction*.

# SNAIL AND THE MER

"*Fish* men," the prince said. He sat up and looked over the ship's side. "Good for eating, I warrant, though little else."

Snail couldn't decide whether he was putting up a brave front or was really that stupid.

*Either way, I must have better eyes than him,* she thought, *or he wouldn't say something so dumb.*

On the near shore, Snail could see that the young Border Lords standing in the shallows had begun thrashing and kicking in the water. Suddenly, one started to scream, high and womanish, before flopping facedown, as if being pulled under by an unseen tide. The others began to beat the water near him with the points of their swords, and one reached down to grab his arm, then backed away frantically.

She saw the flash of an iridescent tail near the fallen warrior's feet. A head lifted that was crowned with eely, green locks of hair. The creature's shoulders, like that of a burly man in his bath, were bare. When it turned its head toward her, Snail could see it had a mouth full of sharp teeth.

All at once, the sea around the young Border Lord's body frothed and boiled, and then suddenly the body was gone, as was the mer, though his wake was pinioned by a shower of spears from the shore.

When the young Border Lord's tam popped up on the water's surface a moment later, his companions set up a loud lament, but none of them waded back in to fetch it, not even the man who'd reached down to grab his friend.

As she watched, something cold and wet, like the slap of a fish tail, seemed to wrap itself around Snail's heart. She started to sit back down when, all at once, she was clutched from behind.

She could feel the coldness for real now. It seemed to begin at the point where she'd been grabbed and radiate around to her front. She gave a little scream, and struck out with the small knife in her hand, even though she knew it would never be enough. Still, when her blade jammed into the creature's arm, the mer screamed like a boggart's wife in labor, a high, awful keening.

At the same time, Aspen took aim at something with his sword, and swung hard, crying, "Duck your head, girl!"

Without hesitation, she ducked, though she was simultaneously being pulled up and out of the boat. Aspen's sword swished over her head but she never heard it connect. Nonetheless, the merman let her go.

The knife must have stayed stuck in the creature's arm, for it was pulled from her hand and was quickly gone, along with the mer, down to the bottom of the sea.

Snail fell forward into the keel of the boat and lay face-down in a puddle of water. For a long moment she didn't dare move, or at least not on purpose, though her entire body was trembling. She didn't think it was from fear. She was well past that and into full-blown terror.

"Girl!" It was the prince's voice.

Even shaken as she was, all Snail could think of was that the toffee-nosed fool could simply not remember her name.

"Snail!" he cried, pulling her out of the puddle and turning her over. "You cannot breathe water, you ninny, so stop trying."

At that she thought, *Ah, I have mistaken him. He does care, though he still talks funny.* She opened her eyes, now befogged with the brine, then blinked rapidly about ten times. When she could see again, she noted that his face was white and shaken.

"How did you *do* that?" he asked.

"Do *what*?" She honestly had no idea what he meant.

"How did you kill the mer?"

"*Kill* it?" How could she have done any such thing? After all, the prince was the one who'd swung a sword at the creature, almost taking her head off as he did so. "But I thought that your sword . . . ?"

He managed to look both shamefaced and alarmed at the same time. "Never connected. It was already . . . gone."

"The sword?"

"The mer."

"*Gone?*"

"Dead."

"*Dead?*" Then she remembered. "I stuck it with the knife. The one I took from the ogre's back." She wondered where the other two knives had gotten to. "But it was such a *small* knife and would have made such a *small* hole."

"The ogre was bigger," he mused.

She nodded.

They stared at one another, before the prince said at last, "But the mer wasn't cut anywhere. Not anywhere I could see. It just seemed to . . . well . . . turn grey and die."

"Same with the ogre," she said.

The Sticksman, in his flat voice, intoned, "Arum."

"Cuckoopoint?" Snail said.

"What *are* you two talking about?" The prince, himself, looked as if he was turning a bit grey.

"Cuckoopoint and arum, one and the same. An herb. A poison," Snail explained. "An extremely *deadly* poison," she added, though she was thinking all the while: *Honestly, princes know nothing about the real world.*

"On the blade?" the prince asked.

All at once Snail's mouth made an O. She grabbed off her apron, bunched it up, though careful not to touch any part of the pocket, and flung it into the river. "Of course! Of course! How could I have been so stupid." She turned and washed her hands in the puddle beneath her, scrubbing as hard as if she were about to help at the birth of a baby. Part of her knew that if she'd been poisoned, she was already well past saving.

She looked up at the prince who seemed astonished at what she was doing. "I could have touched the blade," she said. "I could have cut you when I fell. I could have—" Afraid, ashamed, she broke into tears.

"Look—we are both all right." He held out his hands, palms up, toward her and tried to smile, but it was more grimace than grin.

*Why*, she thought, *he's trying to comfort me. And almost making a job of it! Though Mistress Softhands would never have given him a passing grade.*

As the apron settled on the top of a wave, another merman—this one more silver than green—leapt high into the air as if to avoid the smock, almost hovering above it. He showed his teeth at them and hooted, then dove, effortlessly, back into the sea. But all around the boat, the water boiled for a long moment, and now Snail understood why.

"Stay low," the Sticksman said, his face furrowed as a tree trunk. "I believe they are afraid of you now, lady. They will soon be gone. But till then, best be safe."

*Lady!* Snail thought. *He called me Lady!* It was unthinkable. But perhaps, away from the Unseelie lands, not so unthinkable as all that.

## ASPEN LEADS ON SHORE

*A*spen sat low in the boat, eyes frantically searching the waters. But since Snail had killed the one who had tried to drag her overboard, there had been no more attacks by the mer—no flash of green tail or bubbling froth to signal another assault.

Still, *better caution than a coffin*, his father had always said. So he kept his eyes on the waves and his head continually scanning left and right.

*Left and right*, he thought, then corrected himself. *Fore and aft, rather.* He frowned. *Or is it port and starboard?*

He had never paid much attention to nautical terms, not liking water, boats, or sailors. And he had *never* understood the need to rename directions just because one was on the water. The language of the sailing men that he recalled from his childhood in the Seelie Court was as strange as the trader's dialect, or the gabble of the Border Lords. *Why can they not all speak alike?* he wondered. *Understanding would be greatly improved thereby.*

He snuck a glance at Snail, who was watching the water as anxiously as he. He wondered about asking her what she felt about language but he was not certain how to start the conversation.

*She is nothing like Sun and Moon. Yes, they are cruel,* he thought, *but they know their place in the world and the place of those around them.* He was intimidated by them, infatuated with them, possibly under their spell—but he could certainly talk to them. *Not that they often answered, except with scorn.* But Snail, Snail was so . . . *prickly.* And she certainly didn't know her place. Still, when he had thought her dead, facedown in the bottom of the boat, he had felt . . . bereft.

Suddenly, Aspen heard a grinding sound and the boat stopped with a jerk.

"We have arrived," the Sticksman said. "Get out." As an afterthought, he added, "Prince." It was less a title than part of a command.

Aspen gave a mighty leap over the side of the boat, landing onto a small spit that was half sand and half marsh. Glancing quickly around, he noted that the spit jutted from a thickly forested shoreline into the slow-moving shallows.

*No mer,* he thought, and felt his heart resume its regular beat.

Hearing Snail climb over the side with what sounded like a bit more decorum, he turned just as she landed in the sand. He was surprised at how light she was on her feet.

"But where *are* we?" she asked. "Are we still in Unseelie lands?"

Aspen shook his head. "No," he said.

He was trying to picture the map in Old Jack Daw's apartments, where he had taken lessons in map reading since Jaunty had not thought it worthy of a hostage prince to know such things. "You are not going anywhere," Jaunty had said, "for you must remain here for the rest of your life. And if you go on a hunt, or ride to hounds, the beaters will know where to take you." That had made sense. The beaters were usually wolfmen and they certainly had the nose for the woodlands.

But Jack had disagreed, and said otherwise. "A man *should* know the lands that surround him. A prince *must* know, for he may rule it all some day." And even when Aspen had shrugged and pointed out that he was hardly likely to rule the Unseelie lands, Jack had said, "You have a crystal ball? You are a soothsayer? A seer?" And of course Aspen had had no answer for those questions.

"Are we in Seelie lands then?"

He was so caught up in memory that Snail's voice startled him for a moment. "Not exactly."

"Well, where are we then?" She sounded a bit exasperated. "Your Serenity," she added when he looked up at her sharply.

*See,* he thought, *prickly.* He'd never met a prickly underling before. Except for Jack, of course. Even if he had been only a hostage prince, he was of the highest rank. And the underclasses should know their places. Except, for some reason, this girl did not.

"Well," he said, picking up a short, sharp stick and dusting the sand off of it, "that is not as easy a question as you might think." Kneeling in the sand, he used the stick to sketch what appeared to be the outline of a fat, three-legged squirrel.

"That," he said, tapping the squirrel's body, "is Unseelie land." He scooted a bit to his right and drew a large circle, adding several circles atop and below it. "Those are Seelie lands." He drew a thin line from the squirrel's tail to a spot somewhere in between what might have been rocks or bodies of water. "This is the river path we took." He looked up at the Sticksman, who remained on the boat. "Yes?"

The Sticksman gave a shallow nod. "Yes."

Snail frowned down at the crude map. "Then you know where we are!"

Aspen frowned at his map as well. "Not exactly."

"How *not exactly*?" Snail said loudly. "Don't you *princes* study geography and mathematics and all that?"

Somehow, "princes" didn't sound like a compliment when she said it.

"Well, yes," Aspen said. "But Faerie geography is a tough subject. See here." He tapped the stick on the sand map's Unseelie lands and then the Seelie lands. "The lands held by the two courts are well known and well controlled. We can travel through them freely and easily."

He thought about their narrow escape from the Border Lords and the mer and coughed nervously. "Well, maybe not easily if one is trying to escape. But at least we did not get lost. However, the *unmastered* lands in between have a wild magic all their own and tend to . . ."

"Tend to what?"

"Well, they tend to move around a bit."

"A *bit*?"

"Well, a bit more than that. The Shifting Lands."

Snail sat on the ground next to the map. "Wonderful." She made it sound anything but.

"It is no problem, though. I just have to remember the equations," he told her, though his forehead creased as he tried to recall them. Those had been last year's lessons, after all, and mathematics had never been his strong suit.

Suddenly his forehead smoothed out again. "I've got it!" he said, and he spoke rapidly lest he forget it again. "The elevation of the spot times the number of the season squared gives us the L property that mostly governs the movement factor of forested lands." He smiled at Snail, proud to have remembered such a complex equation. "If we had landed in the plains the calculation is much more complicated." He scrawled some numbers in the sand and then bit his thumb. "I believe we are—"

"You are in the Hunting Grounds," the Sticksman said. He was right behind Aspen, looking down at the map.

"I would have figured that out," Aspen grumbled. "Eventually."

"I don't think we have time for *eventually*," Snail said. "We need to be going *now*."

"Are you not forgetting something?" the Sticksman said.

Aspen looked down and then slapped his forehead. "Of course!" He drew a thin line equidistant from both lands. "The Borders." He frowned. "Though those shift around a bit as well."

"No," said the Sticksman. "My favor."

Aspen gulped. "Ah—that. . . . If it is within my power."

"You will travel far," the Sticksman said. It wasn't a question, and Aspen thought he could feel the power of prophecy in the creature's next words. "And you will meet creatures old, odd, and powerful. You will ask each of them these three questions." The Sticksman waited as if expecting confirmation.

"Um, yes," Aspen said somewhat awkwardly. "And these questions are?"

"What is the Sticksman?" The creature paused not in hesitation but as if setting the words into Aspen's mind. "How did the Sticksman come to be?" Another pause. "How does he come not to be once more?"

"Very well," Aspen said, though inwardly he thought the questions unanswerable.

"If you receive the answer to any of those questions and do not return within a year and a day of learning the answers to share them with me, I shall consider our bargain unfulfilled." The Sticksman leaned very low and fixed Aspen with his pale, pupilless eyes. "Then I would have to seek you out to exact payment."

Aspen did not know how the Sticksman could seek him out or what he meant by "exact payment," but he definitely did not want to find out. Of course, if he never received any answers, then he would not have to return to this shore ever again.

"I am a prince of Faerie and I have given my bond," he said, trying to make the words true by saying them firmly. "A prince and his bond are sacred."

A traitorous thought suddenly came to him: *Is not running from the Unseelie Court breaking the hostage bond?*

But suddenly, for the first time, he realized that *he* had never given his bond. It had been given for him. He had been a child when he was turned over to King Obs and the Unseelie Court. He had had no say in the matter.

*For a man's word to matter it must be freely given,* he thought, *by the man himself.* And he had been no man, but a boy.

"I give you my bond, Sticksman. I shall return with your answers when I get them."

He meant every word.

The Sticksman studied Aspen for a moment more and

then nodded once, apparently satisfied. He turned in a single fluid motion, walked back to the boat, and stepped easily over the high side. Then he stuck his pole in the sand and pushed off. The boat moved off the sand, slipping into the water, and going upstream as easily as it had down.

Aspen knew it would soon be out of sight. But Snail had been right; this was no time for idle watching.

"Come, girl," he said. "It is time to enter the Hunting Grounds."

Then he strode manfully toward the forest, one hand on the hilt of his sword.

He pretended that he didn't hear her when she muttered, "Sure, but are we the hunters or the prey?"

# SNAIL ON THE PATH

*S*nail thought bitterly, not two hours later, that they were neither the huntsmen nor the prey. They were, quite simply, the Lost.

Or as she said to the prince, "We're going in circles."

"How can you know that?" he asked sharply. "*I* do not know that!"

"Because we've passed the same tree three times."

"We have passed a lot of trees. How could you possibly know one from the others?" He spoke witheringly and seemingly without real curiosity.

"Because that's the only tree with the initials BPS."

He looked oddly at her. "I did not see any initials on a tree."

She pointed to a white birch, and there—almost hidden by the leaves—were the very initials.

"You can *read*?" Evidently, that was the thing he was most riveted by.

"Of course I can read. I'm apprenticed to a midwife." She stood, hands on hips, and glared at him.

"*Midwives* can read?" He sounded even more astonished.

She looked at him with the same withering glance he'd given her. "Would you put your darling in the hands of someone who couldn't read the script on a pothecary bottle, leading her to mistake a sleeping potion for, say, *arum?*"

"I . . . I . . ."

It was the first time she'd actually shut him up and it made her grin. She didn't bother to hide her delight.

He squared his shoulders and tried to look princely. Instead, she thought it made him look like a small boy caught pinching butter from the churn.

"So do you know *where* we are?" She gave him a smile, trying for innocence and hitting instead on sass. "Or *where* we are going?"

"I told you these lands tend to move around a bit." Now *he* was getting testy.

She sat down, crossed her legs, and looked up at him.

"What are you doing?"

"If the land moves, then perhaps *we* shouldn't." She held her hands palms up, in mock resignation.

They were in a small clearing facing three paths. The middle one headed deeper into the woods, the left one veered off sharply, the right lazed in a twisty kind of way. Not only was Snail certain they'd been here before, she was also pretty sure they'd taken a different path out each time.

Aspen caught her looking at the paths and said, "*You* choose one."

"Bad idea," she said without hesitation.

He plopped down next to her. "Then what do you propose?"

"I told you: if the land moves, then perhaps we . . ."

This time, he glared at her and said angrily, "I heard you, but that makes no sense, 'Perhaps we shouldn't.' Should not *what*?"

She pointed. "Watch what's happening."

Reluctantly, he looked where she was pointing and his jaw dropped.

The land before them was subtly shifting. As if it was a map writ in water, it moved and changed with a slow, unseen tide.

"How did you know . . . ?" he said, practically in a whisper.

"I didn't. But I guessed." She grinned. "It was a *good* guess, don't you think?"

He stared at the slowly moving landscape. "Knowing doesn't solve our problem."

She smiled, still staring at the shifting land. "Midwives say, *Do not go to the baby, let the baby come to you*."

"Speak plainly!" he said. "*You* are as bad as the Sticksman."

"Let the land show us where to go," she said. And even as she spoke, the land slowed its shifting, and the left-hand path stopped directly before them.

She turned and grinned. "See?"

"Do we dare trust it?"

She shrugged. "Do we have a choice?" Then she stood and reached out a hand.

Reluctantly, he took her hand and she pulled him up beside her. Then she put her other hand in the small of his back and pushed him forward.

"After you, Serenity. I know my place." She didn't even try to hide the fact that she was making fun of him.

He pulled his sword from the sheath and stepped on to the path.

Despite her name, Snail kept pace behind him. Indeed, she didn't dare let him out of her sight.

The first time the path veered sharply left, and steeply downhill, the prince's shoulders went up, and he look angrily over at the gentler slope to the right.

Snail grabbed at his arm before he could step off the path, and whispered, "Think of it as a dance, Serenity. Let the path lead."

"*I* do the leading in a dance," he told her snippily.

She laughed out loud. "I'm sure that in the toffs' grand balls, the men always lead. But in the apprentice dances, anyone who wants to can."

"And chaos ensues," he said sharply.

"Chaos was what we had when we were first in the woods," she reminded him. "When we were going in circles."

He thought a minute, and without actually agreeing out loud, relaxed his shoulders, and let the path take them where it would.

❖ ❖ ❖

FOR A LONG TIME it felt as if they were simply wandering with no apparent destination. By early evening, with no end in sight, the prince was beginning to get nervous. Snail could tell by the way he shifted his grip on his sword, sometimes sheathing it entirely and then, as quickly, unsheathing it and holding it before him.

"We have to find a stopping place," he said. "Gather wood, make a fire, sleep somewhere safe."

"And eat," Snail said, all at once aware of how empty her stomach was. It felt as if she hadn't eaten in days. And then she realized—she actually *hadn't* eaten for quite some time, not since they'd been in the castle and before she was up in the birthing tower. Which had to have been at least a day and a half ago, if not longer.

"*And eat,*" he agreed.

Just as they both came to that agreement, there was a sudden strange sound, as if something was slowly grinding to a halt. They both jerked forward, then stopped walking.

Snail sighed. She suddenly understood that she was not only hungry, she was exhausted as well. The march through the Hunting Grounds and Shifting Lands must have taken longer than she realized.

"I smell something," the prince said, sniffing like a boggart on the hunt.

"What do you . . ." and then she smelt it, too.

Someone close by was cooking cabbage soup.

She spun around but saw no lights, nothing to indicate where the smell was coming from: no campfire, no house, no inn, no castle, no . . .

"Look," the prince said, pointing.

Snail looked through the gloaming, squinting hard to follow his finger.

And there, through the trees, was a dark, round . . . something.

"A *cave*?" she said. "Bad idea."

"I think it's a *good* idea," he said. "It will be warm, keep us safe, and—"

"This place is called the Hunting Grounds, my lord," she said, as if speaking to a child. "Nothing good will live in a cave."

"Someone cooking dinner lives there," he told her.

"What if that someone who lives there is anticipating dinner to walk into his pot?" she asked.

"You do not know that."

"You don't know otherwise."

His stomach growled.

Her stomach growled.

And with that, their fate was decided.

## ASPEN IN THE COOK'S CAVE

The cave entrance was partially concealed by vines and brambles, and Aspen realized how lucky they were to have spotted it.

*If we hadn't looked up at just the right time, we would have walked right past it,* he thought, *even though we could smell it. He wondered idly if the cave had been under some kind of hiding spell. Or if they both had been blinded by hunger and fear.*

"It smells like roasted nuts and honey!" He hadn't had roasted nuts and honey since before he had been a hostage. He could barely remember what they tasted like. But he remembered the smell.

"No it doesn't," Snail said, sniffing the air with a dreamy look on her face. "It smells like cabbage soup. Lovely cabbage soup."

The cave was right before them now, and Aspen had his sword out to push the bushes aside so they could enter.

"No one likes cabbage soup," he told her, but laughed

when he said it so she wouldn't take offense. There was no reason for either one of them to be angry when they soon would have such a wonderful meal.

And Aspen was *sooooo* hungry. He couldn't remember being this hungry since . . . well, since ever.

He stepped into the cave first and was surprised and greatly disappointed when he didn't immediately see a fire or a pan filled with roasting nuts and a pot full of honey nearby.

Checking around in the grey light, he saw that there were a few uncomfortable-looking rough wooden chairs, a table with a broken leg leaning against a wall, a great number of hooks hanging from the ceiling, and one very large, very fat, incredibly ugly troll. Its head scraped the rough stone ceiling, and its eyes were asquint. Two tusks stuck out of either side of its massive jaw. A piece of material covered most of its massive body, but there were holes in various places. Enough, he thought in a befuddled way, to throw a drow through.

However, "Uh . . ." was all he managed to say before the troll pulled back a fist the size of a full-grown pig's head and punched him on the temple. The world went black and he crumpled to the floor.

❖ ❖ ❖

JUDGING BY HOW MUCH his head throbbed, Aspen didn't think too much time had passed before he regained his senses. But what time had passed had been enough for him to be gagged and tied into one of the oversized chairs. He heard a low moan from his right and turned to see Snail similarly trussed up and coming slowly awake.

*Oh, what a fool I've been,* he thought. *Of course, the food smells were an enchantment.* He couldn't have expected Snail to know that. But surely *he* should have.

He wondered if he had grown so used to life in King Obs's castle, with its ward spells against Seelie magic, countermagic that had been layered on for millennia, that he had practically forgotten he had any magic at all. He shook his head—which made his headache all the worse. And now here he and the young woman he should have been protecting had been brought down, sacked, battered, bagged, and captured by that lowest of enchantments—hedge magic. Cast by a troll no less!

He hoped he'd live long enough to be embarrassed.

*I should have known when Snail and I smelled different meals. I should have listened when she warned about going into the cave. I should have . . .* He knew he was not finished shoulding on himself.

He realized that a squirrel coming into the cave would smell an acorn; a rabbit would smell a carrot; a fox, a hen. He had smelled a favorite meal from his childhood. And Snail, no more than a peasant, really, had smelled cabbage soup.

*But seriously,* he told himself, *no one actually* likes *cabbage soup.*

If he had had his wits about him then, he could have

dispelled the glamour easily. But now, with his hands tied and his mouth gagged, there was very little he could do.

*Except get eaten.*

There was a scuffling behind him and then the troll came into view. It was truly, truly fat, its belly protruding far in front of it, pushing the stained cloth it was wearing to the limits of the fabric. He realized it was not just a cloth. It was an apron. There was an embroidered motto on the front he had not noticed before. FEED THE TROLL.

*Honestly,* he thought, *who knew trolls could write? Or that they had a sense of humor.*

The troll's belly stuck out farther than its giant nose, which was now sniffing Aspen from trussed-up head to trembling toes.

"Which first?" rumbled the troll, licking its surprisingly thin lips with a gargantuan tongue. "The sweet, sweet sugar of Seelie Serenity, or the earthy dough of the Fee Fi Foe?" The troll sniffed at Snail before wiping its nose on its apron, which only added to the many stains already there.

At that point, the troll wrinkled its nose as if it had just smelled something it did not like. "The Fee Fi Foe, I think," it said, rubbing its imposing stomach. "The time's coming soon and I need the sustenance. Ohhhhhh!" Grimacing, it pressed a gigantic hand to its belly.

*I think it's in pain,* Aspen thought, a tiny bit of hope growing in his chest like the first thrust of a curled fern in the spring.

The troll stumbled to the far wall where a number of knives and cleavers were hanging. Grabbing the nearest one, it spun back around, its face now clearly showing great pain. By the way it was clutching its belly, the pain was in there somewhere.

*May you fall down and die*, Aspen thought. *May you expire in great pain. May the little hobs eat your innards and crows peck out your eyes.*

He was really getting into the silent curse, which was just as well because mostly he was in a panic and struggling against his bonds. But the rope was strong and the troll's knots held, and he could only watch terrified as the clearly agonized troll stumbled toward Snail, holding its belly gingerly with one hand and a knife almost as big as the girl in the other.

"Snail!" Aspen shouted, only it came out as "Fffffaaaaiiih" because of the filthy cloth stuffed in his mouth.

Snail was fully awake now and was looking at the troll strangely as it approached. She must have been afraid, of course, but mostly she looked . . .

*Concerned?*

Aspen had no time to interpret that look, because he knew she was about to be butchered. Even in the grey light of the cave, the knife gleamed. And the knife wasn't just large, it was huge.

*I have to do something!* Aspen thought.

But struggle as hard as he might there was nothing he

*could* do except watch as the troll stumbled up to Snail, drew back its knife . . .

. . . and collapsed in a heap onto the cave floor.

"Mrrrph?"

"Hurry," Snail said.

Aspen looked over at her again. Somehow, she had worked the gag out of her mouth.

"We've got to get out of these ropes!"

"Mrmm, mrmm," Aspen agreed. He still could not free himself. But the knife had fallen from the troll's hand and was right there in front of him. And if he rocked his chair . . .

It took longer than he had hoped —nine or maybe ten seconds that seemed like an eternity—but he finally managed to rock the chair up onto two legs and then over sideways.

"Owrrrmph!" he grunted as the fall and abrupt stop reminded his head to start pounding again. Ignoring the pain, he wiggled like a one-legged salamander and managed to maneuver himself so his hands were near the knife.

"Yes," Snail said, "just a little more to the left . . . and . . . yes!"

Despite moving only a few feet, Aspen was exhausted by the effort. But he had the knife! It was actually more the size of a Border Lord's great sword, but with his long fingers, he was able to turn it till he had the sharpest edge against the rope. He used his body more than his hands to set up a sawing motion, praying the whole time that the rope would part before the troll woke, or before he sliced off a part of his anatomy. Simultaneously he gave thanks to the green gods for how sharp the troll had kept its knife.

Moments later, the ropes gave way and his hands were free. He cut the rest of his ropes away, and snatching the gag from his mouth—dirty, foul thing!—he turned to the troll. Raising the knife high over his head, he aimed a huge killing stroke at the base of its neck. He knew that trolls were famous for their powers of self-healing, so he'd have to cast a fire spell to seal the troll's death immediately after the deed was done.

"Stop!" Snail shouted at him.

He froze, the giant knife getting heavy over his head. "Um, can it wait?"

"No," Snail said. "We may have only minutes."

"I think we'll have plenty of time once I dispatch this big, ugly thing."

"You can't!"

Aspen looked over his shoulder at Snail, who was still tied into her chair. Then he looked pointedly at the knife. "*You* killed that carnivorous mer. I am reasonably certain that I can kill *this* thing."

She shook her head. "I mean you mustn't." She frowned. "And it's not a thing. It's a *she*. And *she's* pregnant."

Aspen lowered the knife and looked down at the troll. If he had been a true Unseelie prince, he would have just slaughtered her as she lay there, pregnant or not. If he'd had a drop of Border Lord in him, he would have taken pleasure in each cut. But he was a *Seelie* prince, and a Seelie prince does not slaughter females. Especially *pregnant* females.

"Are you certain?" he asked.

"Absolutely positive," she answered.

"Oh, nuts."

The troll moaned and clutched her stomach with both hands.

Aspen leapt back, raising the knife. Since the troll did not move again, Aspen hurried over to Snail and quickly cut her free. He turned to leave, but Snail scampered over to the wall of knives and began examining them.

"Come, Snail!" he hissed. "We must be away now!"

"No, Serenity, we can't. Er . . . mustn't." She seemed to find a knife to her liking, smaller than the rest and maybe cleaner, too.

"I will not kill the awful creature, Snail. That's not what Seelie princes do. But remember—it tried to *eat* us! And if we do not leave soon, it may still succeed."

Snail walked back with the knife and looked down at the troll. "If we leave her, she will certainly die."

"Not our fault," Aspen said.

"It would be mine," she said.

"Why?"

"I'm a midwife's apprentice, Your Serenity. I have taken an oath."

"What oath?"

She put her hand over her heart. As she was holding the knife in that hand, Aspen could not help thinking it odd.

"I swear to help all creatures great and small to give birth in painless peace, by Mab's good heart."

He knew by the way she phrased it that it was a strong and unbreakable oath.

Snail pointed her knife down at the troll. "The baby's clearly breached. See the head up there where it should be down here."

There *was* a peculiar bump in the troll's belly. It might have been a head. Or a foot. Or just a large bump. It might have been something undigested that the troll had eaten the day before. Aspen shook his head.

The troll wife moaned.

"If she doesn't get help soon—very soon—she *will* die." Snail looked up at Aspen and in the grey light of the cave, her bicolored eyes were unreadable. "And the baby, too."

"Nuts," Aspen said again. "Great roasted nuts." Then he sighed. "What do you need me to do?"

She showed him a quick smile then, but as quickly put her lips in a thin line, thinking for a second. "Why, boil water, of course!"

"Of course," he agreed, as if boiling water was the easiest thing in the world in a cave with only an enormous caldron twice his size, no fire, and no water source. "Of course."

## SNAIL'S FIRST BIRTHING

$\mathcal{S}$nail sent Aspen outside to find water. "Remember how odd the land here around is. Let the water come to you." Then she turned back to the pregnant troll.

"I am a midwife," she said to the huge creature, loudly and clearly. "Please remember the law." She meant the one against eating midwives.

The troll nodded.

"Now, let's get you sitting up," Snail said, placing a chair against the near wall, and then helping the moaning troll to sit with her back against the chair's legs.

Snail worried it might be a hard birth. She worried that it might be a cutting birth. She worried the baby might not make it through the canal. But she no longer worried about being eaten. That was the good thing.

And so she set to work.

❖ ❖ ❖

IT SEEMED LIKE only seconds later that the prince was back, though it was clearly much longer. She'd already gotten the troll into the right position, had counted the minutes between the contractions, had taught the creature how to push.

Prince Aspen returned with a clay pot lined with river reeds and mud. It was a coarse first attempt but he seemed proud of his handiwork. The pot was brimming over with water.

Snail thanked him profusely even though she worried about how dirty the water was.

"Not sure how we will start the fire," she said, but he quickly did a piece of princely fire magic, and soon there were flames in the great hearth snapping out what sounded like smart remarks. The pot of water held, and in no time, the filthy water was merrily bubbling away.

She set the knife in the pot in the vain hope that she could cleanse her only cutting implement of any impurities and—she tried not to think of this—any blood from previous troll dinners.

The troll wife groaned.

Prince Aspen turned white, practically glowing in the grey cave.

"Go get me a torch of some kind in case there has to be fine work done," Snail said, thinking all the while that there was nothing fine about delivering a baby troll, nothing at all.

The prince ran from the cave, clearly happy to be out of

there, and Snail turned back to the laboring troll wife. She held the knife in one hand.

"Only if we need it to get the baby out in time," she assured the troll. "So close your eyes, my dear, and push." She sounded a bit like Mistress Softhands and suddenly found herself hoping that the old midwife had fared well and was now herself safely delivered from the dungeon.

Then one hand holding the knife, the other on the troll's massive belly, she began to sing the birthing song over and over. It didn't matter, as Mistress Softhands always said, whether the mother-to-be was an ogre or a queen, the song soothed. Snail tried to lower her voice to match the troll's stentorian tones.

> Arooo, arooo, little mother, and hush.
> Take a big breath and give a big push,
> Child that's within you will soon be without.
> Another big push and then give a great shout!
> Arooo.

Each time she said the word *push*, Snail put pressure on the troll's belly. Each time she sang "little mother," she grinned at the inappropriateness of calling a troll female little.

She sang the song a full ten times and could feel the baby in the troll's belly kicking. And, this being a troll baby, it was a very hard kick.

Arooo, arooo, now toe to head,
Little one, spin around this way instead.
Aroooo, arooo, now head to toe,
Little one, now you are ready to go.
Aroooo.

She could see the outline of the child beneath the skin moving under her direction. Breathing in deeply, she held her breath until the baby was fully turned and no longer breach. The magic—so often practiced but never actually used by her before—had worked.

She let the breath go.

"Soon, soon," she said encouragingly.

The troll wife rolled her great black eyes, and pushed when directed. And on the last push, at the end of the tenth repetition of the song, with a huge shout that rattled the walls of the cave and turned over the pot still bubbling on the fire so the fire itself was put out, a baby troll came hurtling down the birth canal and into Snail's waiting hands. She was so surprised at the speed and the weight of it, she almost dropped it, but for once sense and competence overrode her tendency for accidents, and she clung on to the baby for dear life—his and hers.

"Good girl," she told the troll wife. "Nicely done." Then she cut the umbilical and tied the end in a knot as she had been taught, and slapped the baby on the back.

With that the infant squalled, a sound somewhat between a stallion's whinny and a pig's snort but as loud as an avalanche hurtling down a mountainside.

"It's a boy!" she told the troll wife.

"A boy," the troll said and grinned broadly. The sharpness of her teeth and tusks was not comforting.

*I wish*, Snail thought, *that motherhood had improved her looks, but at least she understands the law.*

Just then, the prince came back. He held out the flaming torch. "See! I have it."

That's when he noticed Snail standing there with the giant baby in her arms, still slippery with birth fluids.

"Give me your shirt, Serenity, so I can cleanse the child."

He shuddered, managing to croak, "Not my shirt!"

Shrugging, she said, "Then take my petticoat and rip it into three pieces."

He set the torch in a holder than had been hammered into the wall, before helping Snail—still holding the baby—step out of her petticoat. Quickly, he ripped it into the strips she needed.

One she used for wiping the child. One for diapering him. And one for covering him up. Then she handed the baby to the troll wife.

"Can we get out of here now?" Prince Aspen said.

"How?" Snail asked, pointing toward the cave opening.

It was already dark outside. Or at least as much of the outside as they could see. The rest was blocked by a huge male troll who was holding up a small rabbit, hardly more than a nibble for such a one.

"Am I late for dinner?" the troll rumbled as he came inside.

24

# WHAT ASPEN BRINGS TO THE BATTLE

When Aspen turned and saw the big male troll, fear hit him as if his heart had suddenly been dunked in cold water. But just as quickly the cold was gone. A sudden wave of heat washed over him, and the strangest thought hit him.

*Finally, a worthy opponent.*

And suddenly he was no longer Little Bit or Weeper or Sniveler—all the names the Unseelie had bridled him with as a child, and that he now realized he had never really let go of. He wasn't even Prince Aspen anymore, a name that *sounded* more regal, but actually came from the time Sun and Moon had seen him quaking at a giant serpent that the Border Lords had captured, shaking, the twins said, "like the aspen's leaves in a stiff wind."

*No*, he thought and then cried out, "I am Prince Ailenbran Astaeri, Bright Celestial, Ruire of the Tir na nOg, and Third Successor to the Seelie Throne." He was a warrior and a warrior-chief-in-waiting. His sword was suddenly in his right hand and the torch he held in his left glowed brighter from the magic flowing from him to its flames. "I am a Prince of Faerie. I am a power mightier than you have ever seen."

The male troll flexed his arms and giant muscles rippled and popped. He flung the rabbit aside and roared at Aspen, who roared right back, matching the giant creature in gusto if not in volume.

Raising his sword high, Aspen began to charge forward, and the troll took a giant step to meet him, arms outstretched to grab, smash, pummel, and destroy.

"Stop it!" two female voices shouted, one high, one very low, and the troll pulled up short. "Don't kill anyone!"

Aspen, however, kept coming and was just poised to take a mighty swing that he knew would remove the troll's head from its shoulders, or at least his huge kneecap from his giant knee, when Snail ploughed into him from the side.

"Oomph," he said, tumbling into a heap beneath her, the torch flung from his grasp. He managed—just barely—to hold on to his sword, and desperately tried not to skewer her.

*Though I probably should.*

"How dare you!" he shouted, struggling to rise.

However, Snail was small, but not slight, and she was peasant-strong.

Aspen could use only one hand to try to get out from under her. He still held the sword and continued to *not* want to stab her with it. *But if she holds me down any longer . . .*

"Huldra!" boomed the male troll. "Tell me true, woman, why don't I kill the intruder?"

"Because they are guests, Ukko." Huldra answered.

"Guests?" Ukko laughed. "They are food!"

"Get off of me!" Aspen hissed at Snail. All the power and magic he'd felt just seconds ago had fled him, and now he was afraid that Ukko the troll would come and step on his head while he was being held down by a mere girl.

*A rather ignominious end,* he thought grimly.

"They are midwives," Huldra said.

"Midwives?" Aspen shouted. That was the final indignity, and with a massive heave, he was able to shove Snail aside. Springing to his feet, he brandished his sword at Ukko. "That is it. I am—"

"A midwife, yes," Snail interrupted. "Or rather, *I* am the midwife." Her hair was wet with sweat and plastered across her face, and she took a moment to tuck it behind her ears. "And I have delivered you a son, Ukko the Cave Troll. A fine son. Big and . . . trollish."

Ukko squinted at her. "Yes, you *could* be a midwife." He turned back to Aspen. "But what is *he*?" His voice roared the suspicion.

Aspen tried to stand straight and tall like the heroes always did in the ballads, but it seemed useless in the face of the troll's great height. He would have brandished his sword manfully at the creature, but he noticed his hand had started to shake and didn't think that would be too impressive. But still his voice held strong as he said, "I am—"

Snail interrupted him again. "He is . . . my . . . er . . . apprentice."

Both Aspen and Ukko turned and stared at Snail.

Aspen found his voice first. "Your *what*?"

"My apprentice," she stated firmly this time. "He was a great help in delivering your son, bringing fire and water as demanded. He used his magic powers to turn the child in the womb." She took a step toward Ukko, putting herself between him and Aspen. "And you know the law against harming midwives." Placing her hands on her hips, she added, "*And* their apprentices."

Her back was to Aspen, but he could picture the glare she must have been shooting at the troll. It made him smile to think of it, and how often she had turned her fierce anger on him the two days they had known one another.

Though Ukko was ten times Snail's size, her glare was causing him to stop and sputter. And that made Aspen's smile even greater.

"But . . ." Ukko waved a big troll hand at the prince's rich clothes and bejeweled sword. "He's a . . ."

"Ah, there is that," Snail said, and Aspen suddenly wondered how she was going to explain his princely attire away.

"He's a seventh son of a lesser royal," Snail began, "and—well—you know the old rhyme, I'm sure." She ran her hand through her hair and Aspen could see that her fingers were trembling. He had heard trolls were nearsighted, and he hoped that was true.

There was a long silence from the Ukko. His jaw had dropped so much, it looked like a cavern. A cavern with teeth and tusks.

Aspen took a firmer grip on his sword.

Suddenly, Snail began to recite in a singsong voice that had little sweetness to it and much desperation.

> One is the heir,
> Two is the spare,
> Three sent away,
> Four for the fray,
> Five for the kirk,
> Six legal work,
> And seven alone
> Must get the work done.

The troll still looked uncomprehending, though the rhyme seemed to have the power of a spell, for his great head rolled from side to side with the rhythm of it.

Aspen felt happy for the small reprieve. Also, he was positive Snail was glaring up at the troll. It was what she did in a tight spot. Perhaps the troll thought that was part of the spell, too. *And,* he thought, *if Ukko can see that Snail has one blue eye and one green eye here in the dark cave, he will probably credit that to magic, too.*

She took a deep breath, then said, "The seventh son. He has to find his own work. And this one, well . . ."

*How stupid can the troll be that he needed every little bit of it explained?* Aspen wondered. *But then, trolls are not known for their brains.*

Snail took another deep breath, almost—Aspen thought—a death rattle. *And it will certainly mean a death if she cannot convince the big ugly fellow that I am* (he shuddered) *an apprentice.*

For a moment he wondered which was worse: death or embarrassment. Only a moment.

"And this one," Snail repeated, "has not once but twice caught a baby before it hit the floor." Another deep breath. "One of them was a mer's child. And you know how slippery they can be."

Aspen could see the troll nodding.

"So he—um—like a good seventh son, *gets the work done!*" Then the rest of it tumbled out. "So his father apprenticed him to a midwife. Me. And part of the training is to seek out places that are far away and to help others for a year under the keen eye of the midwife. We left his father's . . . er . . . castle and, after a year of wandering, found ourselves in your woods and got lost and . . ."

It was clear she was running out of invention and Aspen was not certain he could help her with that any more than he could catch a baby. *But,* he thought, *I will certainly try.* He was about to stand and—*Oberon help me!*—spin more of the preposterous tale, when fate in the form of the troll wife intervened.

"Did you not hear the midwife, husband?" Huldra said. There was a snap to her tone that made Ukko's shoulders tense upward as if they were protecting his ears from being boxed. "She has delivered you a son! And the apprentice helped, too."

Ukko gave Aspen one last angry snarl, then relented. "A son? Let me see this miracle, wife, for didn't the hedge witch tell us you would never bear a child, before we ate her?"

Stepping lightly around Snail, he received the small burden from his mate. "A son," he breathed, and looked back at Snail with such a beatific smile on his face that Aspen was surprised to find he was glad he had not killed the great ugly beast.

"Maybe we ate the hedge witch too soon," mused Huldra.

Aspen thought, *Snail really* must *have powerful magic to make a troll regret a meal.*

"She could have marinated a day or two longer," Huldra added.

"I shall name him . . ." Ukko thought a minute and turned to Aspen. "What are you called?"

Quaking just a little, Aspen took a quick breath and stepped next to Snail. "Ailenbran Astaeri, Bright Celestial, Ruire of the Tir na nOg."

Ukko nodded. It was like a boulder nodding. "I shall name him Og."

"A strong troll name, that," declared Huldra, grinning.

Aspen bowed. "I am honored." He turned and winked at Snail.

"A killing in the birthing room can curse the lives of all involved," Snail said, softly so that only he could hear. "I apologize for the ruse, Your Serenity. If you could just be my apprentice till we leave in the morning?"

"I couldn't poss—" he began, but didn't finish. He knew he should be appalled at her interruption of battle, at her assumption of higher station. He should be angry with her for embarrassing him. He could justifiably have taken her head off for any number of infractions of the laws of royal privilege. But mostly he just felt tired.

Looking at the trolls hugging their newborn and patting its tiny—comparatively tiny—head, he felt the tension leave the cave. He knew that, at least for now, there would be no killing done here. And for that he was completely grateful. And amazingly relieved.

## SNAIL FINDS THE WAY

$\mathcal{T}$he baby cried on and off most of the night, and none of them got much sleep, Huldra least of all.

Ukko had paced half the night, snarling at his wife, and she bared her teeth at him more than a dozen times while nursing the child. Both of them fell asleep at last and snored with a sound as loud as rolls of thunder in the mountains.

Snail and the prince found themselves wide awake because of the noise, staring across the fire at each other. It was like trying to sleep during a battle.

"How do we quiet them?" Aspen asked at last.

"We don't."

"Who could have guessed that having a child was such a noisy occupation," the prince said, not really expecting an answer.

But Snail answered him anyway, between yawns. "That's just the way of trolls." And then she added with a wry smile, "Actually, it's the way of any parents of any newborn. Sleep becomes a privilege, not a right." How often had she heard Mistress Softhands say that. And thinking of Mistress Softhands again, she was suddenly wistful, and thought, *Must be lack of sleep that makes me so . . . so . . . so weepy!*

"If that is true," the prince muttered, "then I shall never have a baby. I prize my sleep too well for that." His face seemed a bit pulled in on itself, as if the lack of the one night's sleep had cost him several years.

She smiled at him again and another yawn came between them. "So I have heard it said in other birth rooms, Serenity. But when you are ready for your own child, you will forget this time." Actually, she'd been in very few birth rooms, but Mistress Softhands had said that often as well.

He shook his head and vowed with great passion, "I shall *never* forget this time." She had no way of knowing if he meant it as a compliment or complaint.

❖  ❖  ❖

BREAKFAST CONSISTED OF some sort of frothy drink that tasted—Snail thought—too much like dirt to be enjoyed. But at least it was wet.

Aspen smiled wanly at Ukko and said, "Good troll, may I ask a question?"

Ukko gawked at him. "Isn't it enough, feyling, that I didn't have *you* for breakfast? Now you must task me with questions?"

Aspen tried a smile, but it barely stretched his lips. It made him look sly rather than honest. "It is but one question, and a small one at that."

The cave was suddenly silent, all of them waiting to hear what Aspen had to say. Even the baby, asleep at last, offered no interruptions, only a tiny series of hiccups.

Aspen drew in a deep breath and then expelled the question in a gust of air: "What is the Sticksman?"

Ukko laughed, a dark hollow sound. The baby stirred but thankfully didn't waken. "Is it a trick question, little man? I am not good at riddles. They make me hungry."

Huldra said, "Everything makes you hungry, husband. Why not ask in return: *What is a Stickswoman?*"

"If I do not care about a Sticksman, wife, why should I care about a Stickswoman?" He stood, hulking as high as the stone roof. "An arguing wife makes me hungry, too!" He raised a fist and Huldra raised hers.

Panic played across Aspen's face. "It is of no matter," he cried, pulling Snail to her feet and pushing her out of the cave.

❖ ❖ ❖

ONCE THEY WERE safely outside, Snail wondered breathlessly, "What was *that* all about?"

Aspen sighed. "About useless," he said and would say no more, though Snail asked a second and then a third time.

At last she stopped asking and they moved away from the

cave entrance where the sounds of the trolls arguing had at last woken the baby, whose hollering drowned out his parents'.

A few feet away from the cave, Aspen and Snail sat down to wait for the paths of the woods to resolve themselves.

They waited.

And waited.

And waited some more.

The prince was clearly unhappy at the wait, standing up and sitting down in quick succession, which, as Snail pointed out, simply made the wait longer. But he couldn't seem to sit still.

At one point during the long wait, Snail asked, "What was happening with—that 'Ailenbran Astaeri, Bright Celestial, Ruire of the Tir na nOg,' stuff? You seemed . . . well . . . pardon me for putting in bluntly . . . out of control. You were babbling about being a mighty power."

"That 'Ailenbran Astaeri, Bright Celestial, Ruire of the Tir na nOg stuff' is just my name. My *full* name." His voice was tight but he looked genuinely puzzled. "And I *never* babble!"

She could feel heat rising in her face. "Serenity, I thought your name was Prince Aspen. I'm sorry if I have offended."

"*Aspen* is my name in the Unseelie Court," he said stiffly. "No offense taken. At least not for that."

*But for other things*, she thought. *Dropping tea on him,*

*tripping and falling against him, almost killing him with a poisoned dagger, calling him her apprentice.* Those *were offenses taken.*

She found herself saying, "I mean, when you saw Ukko in the cave entrance, you grabbed your sword and charged him, calling out your name and power and it frightened me. I was sure that was the end for both of us."

"I do not remember such a thing."

"It was . . ." She was going to say "stupid" and changed that at the last moment to "Truly heroic in a Border Lord sort of way."

His puzzlement turned suddenly to enlightenment. "Ah, Berserker Rage," he said. "It has never happened to me before. Perhaps it occurred this time because I was never before threatened when standing on my own ground."

"So here, in Seelie lands, you are Ailenbran Astaeri, Bright Celestial, Ruire of the Tir na nOg?"

He nodded. "*And* a defender of the realm. Even the third successor to the throne is considered so."

"Even to the death?" She really needed to know in case it happened again.

"I suppose so," he said, then brightened. "Do you know what the name means, then?"

She shook her head.

"It means we are out of the Borderlands now and truly on Seelie soil. Otherwise, even in the grips of a Berserker Rage, I never could have claimed the name. It means we do not need to sit here waiting for the forest to show us the way. We can just head out in that direction where my father's personal lands will be." He pointed to the left.

She bit down on her lower lip, then whispered, "I think you mean *that* direction, Serenity," and pointed to the right.

He looked both ways. "You are questioning a prince on his own soil? You are playing a dangerous game, girl."

She bowed her head. "I don't mean to question, Serenity, but to point out that the troll came from the left. See the tracks? He was hunting but only got a small rabbit. He wouldn't dare hunt on your father's *personal* land where, I'm certain, larger game abounds. Therefore, your father's personal lands must be to the right."

He knelt down and scrutinized the footprints, which, being a troll's, were wide and deep, the toe marks splayed out in a clearly recognized pattern. At last he looked up. "You are right, and I thank you for that, midwife. You have my permission to always give me such good advice, as long as we are not in company."

She thought he sounded a bit miffed, but didn't say so, responding instead with the more conciliatory, "I will follow your lead, Serenity."

❖ ❖ ❖

THE PRINCE TOOK OFF to the right at a run, across a large green sward, and Snail—not much of a runner—was immediately left behind.

For a moment, she lost sight of him where the land rose precipitously, and then saw him again as he crested a sharp hill crowned with silver flowers, and then seemed to disappear.

"Oh no," she cried, but scarcely took time to worry. Puffing and panting, she raced to the hilltop, which, she saw, dipped quite suddenly, which explained his sudden disappearance. But far down at the bottom she could see him again, now a small figure below, his way blocked by a tall, briary hedgerow. He was running full-tilt toward it, sword out, and was immediately trying to hack his way through the briars.

By the time she caught up, he was still hacking in a frenzied manner and getting nowhere.

*More Beserker Rage*, she thought, and watched him for a while before turning her attention to the hedge itself.

At last she called out, "Serenity, put aside your sword. The hedge grows two new branches for each one you lop off."

It took a minute before he heard and understood her, but when he did, he drew a deep breath and began moving backward, a step at a time, until he was by her side. Only then did he really stare at the hedge. There was sweat beading his forehead and he was breathing hard. Such hackwork was hot business.

"Is it true?" he asked, before stepping forward again and lopping off a single branch with great care. As he watched, the hedge produced two new branches, each with twice the thorns of the one they replaced.

He turned to Snail, bowing his head to her. "I beg your pardon, midwife, for disbelieving you. Once again you have saved me." He sheathed his sword.

"Look, prince, look!" she crowed in delight, for as soon as his sword was hidden in its sheath, the hedge parted in the middle as if the fingers of thorn unclasped to offer them a way through.

"Of course, of course," he muttered. "I remember now. It is called a Welcome Hedge. Friends can enter. Those who come with wicked intent cannot. How could I have not seen it? My father promised to have them planted after I left."

Without thinking, she took his hand and pulled him through.

When they were on the other side, he grabbed his hand away from hers. "Do . . . not . . . do . . . that . . . ever . . . again."

She set her hands on her hips and glared at him. "What happened to 'Once again you have saved me'? Is that so quickly forgotten?"

He glared back. "No quicker forgotten than you forgetting your place."

"Well, excuse me, Majesty," she said, and stalked off down the road.

He caught up quickly. "Once again, I have been hasty, midwife. My manners are still Unseelie though I am on Seelie soil."

She let him walk by her side, though they were both silent

for about a league or more. *Anger,* Mistress Softhands once said, *is equally the gag in the mouth of those who have been hurt and those who have done hurt.* Snail gave that some thought as they walked along. But she swore to herself that she would not be the one to speak first.

At last the prince spoke, as if nothing out of the ordinary had happened between them. "Where," he asked, "are the armies? This seems a main road and I see none about."

"Were you expecting them?" She turned and glared at him again as if daring him to be unkind.

"Of *course* I am expecting armies on a main road," he said. "We are at war."

"It doesn't look much like war to me.".

"Nor me," he admitted, as a small goat-drawn cart came into view.

When the cart was next to them, the driver—a farmer's boy—jumped down and gave a head bob to the prince. He was in knee-length breeches and braces, and a broad-brimmed hat made of straw that perched on his head with as little effort as a songbird on a limb. "May I offer a ride, my lord?"

Aspen leaned forward. "Have you heard of the Sticksman?"

The boy looked bewildered. "Sticks? Man?"

"Never mind," Aspen said, shrugging. "You are not old or odd or powerful."

"No, sir." If anything the boy looked more bewildered than before.

"Yet still, I have asked and you have answered."

Now the boy no longer looked bewildered, but nervous, as if not having the proper answer to a lord's question might be dangerous. "Can you ask me something else, lord?"

"Stop toying with him," Snail said sharply.

Aspen sighed. "All right. Here's a question you can surely answer. Do you go to the palace?"

Eager to please, the boy grinned. "Yes, sir, that I do. With five kegs of muddled cider, my mam's specialty. The queen loves it."

"The queen?" Aspen began, his eyes suspiciously looking a bit watery, like petals after a heavy dew.

"We accept," Snail said to the boy, giving the prince some time to pull himself together. "I'll come up front with you."

They got in, Snail sitting next to the boy and Aspen perched precariously on a slat bench in the back.

Snail spent the first part of the journey asking the boy about his family, then questioned him about the king's family, and finally, tentatively, the state of the war.

"Not been a war about here in Seelie land for . . . well for longer than I've been alive," the boy said.

"Well . . . I heard . . ." Snail began, then immediately shut up. There was something here that needed thinking about, not speaking about. Even to the prince. She turned her head to see what he'd heard.

But Aspen had fallen fast asleep, as if after the long and

difficult night in the troll's cave, the battle with the hedge had exhausted him completely.

She turned back to the farm boy. "And may it stay that way for all the rest of the years of your life. And mine." Though she was not sure if by saying it she was making a wish or laying a curse.

Either way, the farm boy seemed pleased with her statement, and in companionable silence, they made the rest of the blessedly short trip to the king's castle.

## ASPEN IN THE CASTLE

*The* cart hit a rut and Aspen's head bounced against the shoulder he had fallen asleep on. Opening his eyes with a start, he realized the shoulder had been Snail's. He wondered when she had climbed in back, and he glanced at her guiltily. She was staring at him with an expression he could not read. He tried to figure out something to say, but failed to think of anything appropriate.

*Thank you for your service as a pillow? Sorry for drooling on your shoulder?*

The thank-you seemed overly formal for two boon traveling companions; the apology not warranted considering their relative stations. He refused to embarrass himself either way, but still worried about the right thing to say. For some reason, talking to the apprentice midwife was more difficult than talking to the princesses Sun and Moon.

*And by Oberon! That was difficult enough.*

He was saved further struggle by Snail speaking up first.

"Is that . . . ?" she began, pointing up the road.

Aspen followed her gaze and saw Astaeri Palace rising up over the horizon. The seat of the Seelie Court had been built to be impressive when seen from any angle, but approaching from the main road it was especially inspiring. While the Unseelie capital fortress was frightening in its sheer martial hugeness, Astaeri Palace inspired with sweeping arches and sky-thrust towers. Its walls were bone white, its windows mirrored, its roofs tiled in blue and green. There were golden gutters called eaves troughs and bronze gargoyle rainspouts long gone green. From the tops of the many towers, with their bronze top hats, also greened over, brightly colored banners fluttered halfway to the horizon. In the gardens decorative fountains shot cascades of water high into the air to sprinkle the huge topiaries based on creatures both real and imagined.

"Yes," Aspen said, "Astaeri Palace." But he was thinking, *Home*.

Snail eyed the palace critically. "It's a bit much, don't you think? All those statues and towers and . . ."

"I suppose it would certainly seem so to a *servant,*" Aspen replied haughtily. But he immediately regretted the angry words when he saw the look on Snail's face, part anger and part pain. He was certain it would turn to a glare in a moment. He wondered why he should care. He put it out of his mind, and squared his shoulders, calling to the farmer's

lad in the front seat in as imperious a tone as he could mus-
ter, "Go, boy! Now! Go!"

Surprised, the boy clicked his tongue against the roof of
his mouth, slapped the reins against the goat's back, and the
creature startled and sprang forward.

Snail had to grab on to Aspen to keep from falling out.
He decided to say nothing this time, thinking only that
now they were even, and he need not worry about offend-
ing her again.

❖ ❖ ❖

THE RIDE UP the long road to the castle was straight, and
eventually the goat slowed back down to its original pace.
Of course it was not as strong as one of the oxen back in
the Unseelie Court, nor even as strong as their warhorses.
*Though*—and Aspen chuckled when thinking of it—
*warhorses would never be put into traces to pull. As soon marry
a dairy maid to a prince.*

Finally, still a good half a league from the castle, the goat
stopped altogether, but the prince, in his joy to finally be
home, forgot all decorum and grabbed Snail by her hand
and dragged her from the cart.

"Thank you, good peasant," he called to the goat-cart
boy, hoping Snail heard him using the P word without
scorn, "we will go the rest of the way by foot."

They moved quickly along, not speaking at all, saving

their breath. Not even when they passed handcarts piled high with vegetables in withy baskets. Or passed others filled with woven goods drawn by spavined horses whose knees knocked together. They were silent the whole way, for Aspen's eyes were on the castle, though he kept hold of Snail's wrist as if she were some sort of prize he dared not lose.

When they were almost to the tall wooden gate studded with bronze spikes, Aspen could no longer contain himself. He began running toward the palace, pulling Snail along with him.

"Wait, I can't run that fast!" Snail complained, but Aspen just laughed, running faster, never letting go of her wrist.

"Come, Snail, you must not keep the lords and ladies waiting for me." And then in sheer exuberance, he just shouted one word, the important one: "Home!"

Workmen, traders, peasants, and peddlers all shuffled off the road to make way for the crazed boy, most shaking their heads at the folly of both royalty and youth.

"Good morrow!" he called to them, and "Good E'en," and "Good whatever!" and began laughing even harder when he realized he had no idea of the time. Nor did he care that he did not know. Being home whatever the time was all that mattered.

And finally Snail was laughing with him. Wriggling out of his wrist hold, she grabbed his hand and held it tightly,

as if they were of the same class and she had every right to
do such a thing.

Aspen realized with a pleasant jolt that he was happy for
the first time in as long as he could remember. Not just a
little bit happy, but totally happy.

They reached the gates panting and giggling and full of a
kind of giddy relief.

Stopping suddenly, Aspen pulled sharply on Snail's hand
and slipped out of her grasp. He looked up into the stern
face of a young captain of the guards. Two more guards
stood close behind him. Their uniforms all had gold but-
tons and bangles shining so brightly in the sun. They were
hard to look at.

"Good whatever, Captain," Aspen chuckled while Snail
performed what he realized was a true courtly bow.

*Perhaps some of my manners have finally rubbed off on her.*

"What is the meaning of this?" barked the captain, no
trace of humor in his voice.

*There's something about that voice, that face . . .*

Aspen took a closer at the guard's face and a wide grin
jumped to his lips. "Why, Gann! Do you not recognize me?"

Gann peered down at Aspen, who waited patiently until
the spark of knowledge lit Gann's face.

"By the ancient trees, Bran! Is that you?"

"Yes, brother, it is," Aspen answered. Then he was
engulfed in the older boy's arms and he hugged him back.

Both their shoulders were wet from tears, but their eyes were dry when they released the hug, both holding on until they had gotten their emotions under control. The other guards glanced away and made no comment.

"Mother will be overjoyed." Gann held Aspen by the arms and looked at him. Frowning, he said, "You look hard-used by your travels. Did those Unseelie blackguards not send a proper escort when they released you? And when did they release you? I had not heard word."

Aspen shook his head vigorously. "They did not release me, brother. I escaped. With war starting, I was to be executed."

"*War?*" Gann scoffed. "There has been no hint of war."

The guards behind him suddenly leaned into the conversation.

"But, I was told . . ."

"You were told wrong." Gann's voice was oddly cold.

The guards' expressions suddenly changed as if they were suddenly on high alert. Their hands on the hafts of their spikes turned white at the knuckles.

Aspen couldn't fathom it. Jack Daw had told him . . .

*Jack Daw had lied.*

The enormity of what the old drow had done hit Aspen like a troll's fist and his knees buckled. It was Snail who grabbed his arm to steady him, and for once he did not shake her off.

"I . . . I . . ." he said, but couldn't think of what to say further.

"We need to speak to Father." Gann's face gave nothing away. But his voice was no longer that of a brother's. He sounded like a distant stranger. An enemy.

Aspen nodded mutely and, guided by Snail's hand, trudged into the palace he had been ready to skip into just moments before.

❖ ❖ ❖

THEY WALKED DOWN the long, polished halls and Aspen did not try to look around, remembering, but rather stared ahead as if to be certain he did not trip and fall. He wanted to be princely, stately, brave, for whatever lay ahead.

*I will not think about it*, he thought, though he could not help thinking, worrying, gnawing at the worry like a dog on an old bone, looking for meat where there was none.

When at last they entered the throne room, they were marching at a morose and slow pace, like a tiny funereal procession, just the five of them in order: Gann, Aspen, Snail, and the two guards from the gates. Aspen thought Gann had given the guards some kind of signal, for they had spread out a little, grasping their weapons in a way to be a little more ready.

*As if I am a prisoner, not a returning son.* Which, he supposed, he might be.

Unlike Gann, the queen recognized her youngest child at once.

"Bran!" she shouted. "Oh, my dearest Ailenbran!" She leapt off her throne and started toward him.

"Halt!" shouted the king. "What is the meaning of this?"

But his mother did not halt. Instead, she ran to his side and drew him to her with her left hand, the heart hand, to signal their connection, though not quite embracing him because they were, in fact, in the company of others.

His mother. She who had been so tall when he left was now shorter than he by several inches, though otherwise exactly as he remembered. Her thin features, softened by her kind nature, were still beautiful though centuries old. She had long red hair piled on her head in complex braids, and green eyes that had been written about in ballads because they were so unusual.

On the other hand, his father was sitting on the throne with his shoulders hunched, leaning forward and scowling—which was not what Aspen remembered of him. The king was extraordinarily fleshless for so powerful a man, and short for an elf, as if the crown weighed him down, stunting his growth. It looked especially heavy on him now as he frowned at Aspen, lips thin and bloodless beneath the white moustache.

Gann seemed about to speak, but Aspen stepped in front of him.

"I have returned, Father," he said.

"Yes, I see that." The king stood and looked about to step down from the dais, but quickly stopped himself. He shuddered slightly.

*A mountain trembling,* Aspen thought.

"But why, boy?"

Aspen slipped the leash of his mother's grip and moved a step closer to the throne. "I was told that war was upon us."

"You were *told* . . . ?" The king sat back down heavily. "Oh, Son, would that I had warned you of politics. But you were so young, and I thought they would not—could not—involve you." He ran a hand through his thinning hair. Aspen was surprised to see how pink his father's scalp showed beneath the white hair.

His father went on. "Still, Obs is not clever enough for this . . ."

"Jack Daw." Aspen spit out the name as if it soured his mouth.

The king nodded. "Oh yes, Old Jack Daw. Peace always sits uneasily on that one's shoulders. He is not so different from the rest of his drow clan. They eat their nest mates, you know. He has often come here to court to report on your condition and to try and foment rebellion against me. Only his status as Obs's envoy has kept him safe from my assassins. This is his kind of game exactly."

"Obs's envoy?" *Jack had never told me any of that.* "I thought he was my friend."

"You had no friends in that place. Would that I had warned you of that."

"You may have, and I forgot," Aspen said, wanting his father to have no guilt about what had happened, yet in a deeper part of his mind, wishing to make him feel guiltier.

"You were too young to understand. I said nothing."

"So then, Father, what does this mean? I only came here because I wished to avoid execution." Aspen tried to keep his voice even, but he knew it was on the verge of breaking. As was he.

He tried to meet his father's eyes, but the king looked away. So too did his mother, for she was busy giving the king a look that was half fury, half pleading.

"Do you not see, Son?" the king said, more to the wall than to Aspen. "You have brought the very thing you wanted to avoid upon yourself. And you may have doomed us all as well."

For the first time, Aspen thought of something other than his own fate. Had he, indeed, a prince of the Seelie folk, brought disaster to his own realm? He could not believe it was true. He could not live should it be true.

Not being privy to Aspen's inner thoughts, the king now spoke to Gann not as his son but as the captain of the guards. "Ailenbran is your prisoner. He has brought war to a land woefully unprepared for it and has traitorously broken his word to his monarch. And as that injured monarch, I must do as the law prescribes."

Looking aghast, Gann just nodded. The two guards stepped to either side of Aspen and grabbed his arms roughly.

"Father?" Aspen said, not trusting his voice to say anything more.

"I do remember telling you this one thing long ago, Son," the king said, almost too softly to hear. "Perhaps you have forgotten. *War does not call, it commands.*"

"*Even kings and queens must do as it demands,*" Aspen finished for him.

His father finally met his gaze and Aspen dared him to look away. "And now it *demands* my life?"

The king did not move or speak for a short few moments, then finally nodded. "It is the only thing that may stop the war. A war we cannot win."

"Is that certain, sir?" Aspen managed to keep the terror out of his voice, and that surprised him.

"The armies are not ready. The mages are not ready. The people are not ready."

*And* I *am not ready*, Aspen thought, but kept that to himself. Instead he asked, "But the Unseelie are?" He already knew the answer.

"You can wager that Jack Daw would not have made this move otherwise."

Aspen thought desperately. "But what of your Unseelie hostage, Prince Nobo?"

The king shook his head. "You have killed him as well if Obs marches to war."

Aspen nodded. He looked around the throne room. It looked much smaller than he remembered. But then again, *he* had been much smaller the last time he had been here. "My life has never been my own, has it?"

"That is the curse of rule, Ailenbran," the king said. "We serve the people even more than they serve us." He spoke over Aspen's head to Gann. "Take him to the dungeon. And his companion as well. She will hang with him."

"What?" With a great heave, Aspen shook off the arms that held him. He stopped short of drawing his sword. "No, sire! If it is the curse of rule, then I shall do what I must for the good of the kingdom and the people." He looked at Snail, who, he was overjoyed to see, was glaring at the king for having the gall to condemn her. "But she rules nothing."

The king shrugged. Aspen thought it a very unkingly gesture. "What of it? She traveled with a traitor, she must die with one."

"Father, grant me this boon. She knew nothing of this. She may have been helping a traitor. But she did not know that. She thought she was helping a friend."

Snail shot him a look as he said that. For once her glance was soft, not glaring. He wondered if he dared call her a friend. He had never had one before. He wondered if a prince could befriend . . . It was too hard to think about.

Turning back to his father, he said, "Grant me this boon, sire, and I will go to my fate knowing that I did one thing right in my short time in this land."

The king stared at Aspen as if seeing him for the first time. Then he stood and bowed deep and low. "You are truly noble, young sir, and I am proud to call you my son." To the guards he said, "Take him away. The girl goes to the kitchens for employment."

"I am a midwife, Majesty," Snail protested.

He waved her away. "You are not a midwife in this land."

## SNAIL'S TIME OUT

*J*t took only one guard to show Snail the kitchen, but he was enough. His very presence, the sharpened pike, the sword at his side, the dagger in his sock, the fact that she didn't know her way around the palace's twisty halls, all ensured that she did not try to escape.

He spoke little to her except to bark out instructions like *Right! Left! Down those stairs!* And all done in quick-march time.

She said nothing in return, but followed everything he told her to do. She feared what would happen if she didn't. Along the way, she stumbled twice, and each time he grabbed her roughly by the shoulder and righted her. She could still feel his fingerprints burning her shame and fear into her skin.

As they walked—trotted, actually—she marveled at how much the Seelie castle did—and did not—remind her of the castle at the Unseelie Court. There, of course, she knew every level, from the basement dungeons to the turrets. She knew the turning of every walkway. Had known them from childhood up.

*Well, not* every *bit of it,* she reminded herself. She'd never been in the royal chambers or the council chambers. Or the constable's lodgings. But she knew the girls who cleaned all of those, and she certainly knew *where* the places were and how to get there. And she *had* had a peek into the guards' quarters once, before escaping from an overamorous and slightly drunk young guard, who, the very next day, she saw in manacles being paraded around the yard. For being drunk on duty, not for trying to snatch a kiss from an accident-prone apprentice midwife, of that she was sure.

This castle had dungeons, in one of which Prince Aspen was currently residing. *Though residing is a strange way of putting it.* And a throne room. And hallways and stairways and airways—those narrow arrow slits in the walls. Exactly like King Obs's palace. But this one was also, somehow, lighter, fancier, less military, less . . . she struggled to think of the word, then had it. *Less overpowering.*

In fact, it seemed an inviting place.

Or it *had* seemed an inviting place until the king had thrown his own son in the dungeon because Aspen had tried to escape being executed by the king's own enemy, which—to Snail—made no sense. But when did the toffs make sense? They just made gold, made merry, and made war. And the ones who suffered were the underfolk.

*All right, so it had seemed inviting until I was sent to the kitchen*, she thought sourly. *But that's still better than being in the dungeon.*

❖ ❖ ❖

THE KITCHEN WAS on the lowest level and built, the guard explained, into the hillside. So there were windows on one side, overlooking a sheer drop down to a deep, black lake. The other side of the kitchen was a simple wall. Simply stone and simply several feet thick throughout.

The guard pointed toward the lake. "Dragons," he said. He had a voice that seemed filtered through his rather large and rather bulbous nose.

Being Unseelie and used to hearing about awful things the Seelie folk had, Snail believed him.

"Very fast, very mean, very hungry dragons."

She believed that, too.

"So don't try to escape, girl. There's only the road. We guard the road."

"I thought I wasn't a prisoner," she said, "just kitchen help."

He grunted, which wasn't an answer. Or perhaps it was. She couldn't be sure.

The head cook came over to see who she was.

"King wants her here," said the guard. And then he turned and left. It seemed all the instruction he'd been given and—having passed it on—he was done with his duty.

The head cook looked like a pale dumpling, his face and body in doughy folds. His eyes were black raisins, his mouth strangely red, like a berry plumped into that doughy white face. "What do you know about kitchens?" he asked. It was like hearing an uncooked dumpling speak.

"I know how to eat," she said.

"Hmmmmmmmfff!"

"I am an apprentice midwife," she added.

"No use for a midwife in the kitchen." The berry mouth turned sour.

"I'll be sure to mention that to the king when next I see him," Snail said.

"King wants you here, here you stay," he told her, unaware that she had tried to make a joke. "Just keep out of my way, and out of the way of my cook boys, pot boys, and serving boys."

She looked around and noticed the bustle of pot boys toiling at the stone sinks. The cook boys, too, were hard at work within the ample jaws of the two arched fireplaces, where—she was sure—whole trees could have been burned for cooking meat. It was too early in the day for many serving boys to be about. But except for her own presence, there were no other females in the kitchen, not at all like the kitchen in the Unseelie Court where half the servers and some of the cooks were women and girls.

Before she could wonder further, the head cook said,

"Remember, stay out of my way or I'll stick an apple in your mouth and serve *you* for supper!"

She believed him, too.

❖ ❖ ❖

TWICE DURING THE afternoon she'd tried to head for an open door and both times was stopped roughly. The first time was by a pot boy who—alerted by a server—tripped her, and she fell, bruising her shoulder.

The other time happened when she noticed that no one was watching her. She strolled slowly and casually in a large circle around the central carving table as if just stretching her legs. She'd almost reached the door when a pot was hurled—she never saw who threw it. The pot hit her in the back of the head and felled her as if she was a pin in a game of tall pins.

She didn't try to escape a third time. After that, she just sat on the perch she was given and tried to stay awake.

Now, all Snail's life she'd been busy, whether she did a job well or poorly. She had never been left on her own. But here she'd nothing to do except worry about getting in the doughy cook's way, worry about being served for supper, and worry about Prince Aspen. All that worrying almost drove her crazy. So, she did the only thing she could—she fell asleep.

When all the kitchen work was done, the boys all off to

bed and the tapers and lanterns and torches snuffed out, the doughy cook, with the last taper in hand, noticed her, dozing in the corner.

"Girl!" he said, poking her with a wooden spoon as if he'd sully himself if he touched her with a finger.

She opened her eyes.

"You sleep here. I will lock you in."

"But . . ." she began. At home she had a bed, a place to bathe, covers.

At home she had a candle by her bedside and a cup of water. At home . . .

And then she remembered that if she were at home, she would be in prison awaiting execution. Or she might have already been executed and awaiting burial. Or already buried and awaiting worms.

She shuddered and said nothing more, simply watched as he went out, and then breathed a sigh when she heard the three clicks of his keys.

For a minute she thought she would be crushed by the dark in this unfamiliar place. But then she saw that through the narrow windows she could see the stars.

And the moon.

They were a comfort of sorts.

She found the stub of a candle and managed to light it with an ember from the remains of the fire in the left-hand hearth.

❖ ❖ ❖

THREE TIMES SNAIL went around the room, seeing what she could in the candlelight, worried that the candle would burn out before her tour of the place was done. But then she found four more candle stubs and lit them one after another from the first.

The room was too solidly built, the windows too narrow to slip through. And even if she could get through, she was too high over the lake and would be killed in the fall. And even if the fall didn't kill her, and even if she could swim across the lake, there were those pesky dragons.

*So*, she thought, *escape is off the menu*. Though, she feared, she might still be on.

It was then that she saw something odd and shining in the right-hand fireplace, the largest of the two. Going over to examine it, she kept losing the light each time she put her hand toward it. Only at the last moment did she glance up and there, way at the top of the vast chimney, she saw what was casting the light. The moon was shining down, for at the moment it was right over the chimney opening.

She knew the moon rode across the sky at night, following its sister sun. Could she climb up the inside of the chimney with the moon as her guide?

*Is it possible? Is it dangerous?*

She thought: *Surely chimney cleaners managed. Those sooty fellows who came around twice a year, spring and fall with their apprentices and ropes. With their funny way of speaking, and strange songs.*

She couldn't hope to be as fast or as knowledgeable as they, but it was all that she had.

Racing back to the sinks, she found several large knives set out to dry for morning use. She grabbed up two and tied them with twine around her neck. She also tied two of the candle stubs—the other two had already burned down to puddles of wax. The twine was sufficient for tying the knives but not strong enough for a climbing rope.

Still, it was then or never. She ran back to the chimney, but a bit more carefully because of the knives around her neck, and felt around till she found some stone steps jutting out.

Slowly, with infinite care, she started to climb.

She was about fifteen steps up, when the stone juts stopped and she realized she was barely halfway up to the top, and the moon had already moved a quarter of its bulk off the chimney opening.

"No," she whispered to herself, then louder, "*Nooooooooo!*"

She was making too much noise to hear the sound of the door opening below, and too far up in the surround of stone chimney. But when a woman's voice came halloing up, calling "Girl? Girl!" Snail was so startled, she could have fallen down, which would surely have killed her, but luckily she was standing with her back firmly planted against the chimney wall.

"I will get you out of here," came a voice. It was soft and strong at the same time, and so convincing, Snail was ready to climb down at once. She was tired of being without help, and here was help offered. Only later did she realize that she'd been bespelled.

She untwined the knives from her neck and dropped them into the echo chamber of the chimney, and followed them but slowly, backing down each stone step until she was at last on the chimney's floor. Then, picking up the knives, she turned.

The queen stood there, a lantern in hand.

Snail knew then that she could trust her entirely.

"I will get you out and set you on the road, girl. It is the least I can do for my son."

"Snail, Majesty, they call me Snail."

"Not any kind of name for my son's only friend," the queen said. "I shall call you Nomi instead. It means *'loyal one'* in the Old Tongue. You must use it for your escape."

"Nomi," Snail said, though she was thinking, *No-me. Not me.* And indeed, in the queen's presence, she did not feel herself at all.

The queen nodded at Snail, the very smallest gesture, barely perceptible. In return, Snail dropped practically to the floor in a deep curtsey. "I will try to be worthy of the name, Majesty," she said.

❖ ❖ ❖

THE QUEEN LED HER to a hidden passage through the wine cellar and thence through the walls, their way lit by only the lantern the queen carried, which threw awful shadows—some short as foxes, some tall as dragons.

*All,* Snail thought, *seem to have teeth.*

When they finally reached a door, the queen stopped and handed the lantern to Snail.

"Here, Nomi, hold it high."

Snail did as she was told, and the queen took a large chain from around her waist, on which hung about three dozen keys. She fit the smallest into the keyhole and opened the door. Once it was open, the queen took the lantern back.

The cool air and the smell of freedom was as filling as a meal. Snail breathed it in and out several times.

"There," the queen said, pointing, "go east toward the rising sun, and quickly, but do not run or otherwise call attention to yourself. There you will find a royal graveyard. Look for the tomb of the kings. You can say your good-byes there."

"Is he gone then?" Snail asked, her eyes unaccountably filling with tears. "Is the prince gone? So soon?" She wondered that she'd felt nothing—no tremor, no cold around the heart—whenever the moment of his death had been. *Not much of a friend, then!* she thought.

"Gone," the queen said, her voice low but without a single quaver.

Snail was surprised at how little the queen seemed affected by her son's death. Of course, the queen hadn't actually seen him since he'd been seven years old and surely the Unseelie queen would have acted just as coldly. Both of them had an army of servants to raise their children. Not like ordinary folks who actually dandled their babies on their knees. Even the trollwife had fed the child herself, not needing a milk nurse to do the job for her.

"I shall say a prayer to Mab for his soul," Snail whispered, and surprised herself by meaning it.

The queen said nothing in return but simply pushed Snail out of the door, then locked it behind her.

Snail heard the *snick*, and then the path unfolded before her. She took one step, then another.

Pausing to look at the large brooding castle behind her, Snail told herself she was glad of the escape. But then another thought crossed her mind. *I left him to die alone.*

It didn't matter that she'd had no choice. That the king had commanded and the guard had obeyed. All that mattered was that Prince Aspen had died and she hadn't been there as witness, to lend him some kind of strength.

She began to weep, but as the sun was already touching the horizon with a red glow, she knew she would have to get going before someone came into the kitchen and discovered that she was gone.

So, still weeping, she headed east, walking quickly but not running, as the queen had commanded, letting the freedom beneath her feet begin to heal her pain.

❖ ❖ ❖

THE SUN WAS barely over the horizon when she got to the royal cemetery, its stone monuments like teeth in a beryl green mouth.

Near her was a tall stone tree on which a verse was carved.

> Unveil thy heart, thou faithful tomb.
> Take this new treasure to thy trust,
> And give this baby princess room
> A while to slumber in the dust.

"Poor mite," she whispered. It mattered not if it were a baby princess or any baby, the loss made her sad.

Farther on, an ornately carved tombstone in the shape of a harp, read:

> Here lies the fair maid of the east
> Who loved the souls of man and beast,
> But beastly indeed was the fever.
> Only her harp did never leave her.

She wondered if that meant they'd buried the harp with her, which seemed a shame. A good harp was difficult to make.

But she didn't see any mention of kings on the close-by tombstones. Snail guessed that the kings and queens weren't buried under these simpler headstones, but in the chapel that she could see was at the end of the path, an elaborate thing that looked like a little castle.

She hurried toward it, and when she was close, saw that it had green men and dragons entwined in stone on the columns. But she hesitated to go in. Aspen wouldn't be buried in there. He was a third child, not a king, and died as a traitor. Surely the queen meant something else.

Glancing about for some newly turned earth that would signal a newly dug grave, she found it on the far edge of the graveyard. She ran toward it, tears again in her eyes, and so didn't see that there was a huge lump of overturned soil in her way. She stumbled and began to fall, the open gravesite yawning before her.

Something grabbed her arm and kept her from tumbling six feet down, probably landing on her head.

"Are we even in the rescuing race yet?" asked a familiar voice.

She turned, gasped. "But your mother said you were gone."

"So I am," Aspen told her. He was dressed oddly in multicolored rags and a red floppy hat with bangles hanging from it. He should have looked ridiculous, but he looked older somehow. Graver. Steadier. Snail didn't think it was the clothes.

"My mother convinced me, in between her tears, that my death would not actually stop the war," Aspen said. "In fact it might further provoke it." He frowned. "Though now I do not see how it could. My mother . . ."

"She's very convincing, your mother," Snail said, as Aspen's voice trailed off. She remembered the queen's voice coming up the chimney. "I thought she meant you were dead, when she said you were gone."

"And so we should be . . . gone on the road," he said. "It was Mother who found me this minstrel outfit. I have fresh clothes for you, too."

"I don't need . . ."

"It is a *disguise*," he said. "You cannot be wandering the road as a midwife. That is what everyone will be looking for."

"But that's what I *am*," Snail said, "just as you are a prince. And what will we be if we are not those people?"

"We will be dead." His voice was like a sword at the throat. "And dead we will not be those people either, and with no chance to be any other."

"But . . . but . . ." She wondered why she should suddenly be sniveling about this when what he said made perfect sense.

"So you see, that is why I am not a prince now, but a minstrel, a wandering troubadour, a thing of song and patches." He waved his hand airily, but his voice still held that princely snootiness. She guessed there was no disguising that.

"Well, can you sing?" she asked.

"No, I was hoping you could. I play the lute. It may be my one accomplishment."

She suddenly saw he was holding a modest instrument in his other hand, not nearly as ornate as some lutes she'd seen, with only a cherub carved in the top end, and badly carved at that. For one thing, it was cross-eyed, and for another, its nose was smashed, as if it had been in a fistfight.

"I can't sing, but I *can* pass the hat, Serenity." She looked at him dubiously.

"It will do," he said. "And you will have to call me Karl."

"Karl?" She smiled. "It suits you about as well as those clothes."

He grimaced. "Which is to say not at all. But the name, like the clothes, will have to serve."

"I'm Nomi."

"Loyal?" Aspen grinned. "I see my mother's hand in that."

She handed him one of the two knives. "Your mother is . . ."

"Yes, she is," he said, and grinned.

❖ ❖ ❖

SHE CHANGED INTO the new clothes behind the chapel with the prince—*Karl*, she reminded herself—standing watch at the front. The gown his mother had sent along was of a soft mauve wool with lace collar and cuffs. It was more elegant than anything she'd ever owned, more like something a lady's maid might have worn, or a minstrel's minion. She doubted it would wear well on the trail.

Gone, too, were the striped stockings, and in their place she put on the dull black ones that he'd handed her. The shoes were still her own. The ones the queen had sent were too small and not made for walking. But she tied them around her neck by their laces in case she could barter them at a market town for something more suitable.

The midwife wear was too easy to identify, so they buried it in the open grave under a shower of loose dirt and stone. With luck, a coffin would soon be set down upon it and the grave closed for all eternity.

And with that they were off, weaving their way through the old monuments, and back into the living world.

It was now full day, the sun lightning the sky and with nary a cloud to shadow it, so they would have to be careful.

## ASPEN LEADS THE WAY

Snail followed close behind Aspen, apparently trusting his knowledge of the countryside to lead them. It made him feel almost like a hero from the old nursery tales Lisbet had entertained him with way back when.

The feeling lasted about two minutes.

*I don't know why I should feel heroic,* he thought bitterly. *All I have done is carry us from one disaster to the next. And I do not even know where we are going.*

Sighing heavily, he stopped and turned to look at Snail.

"I have no idea which direction we are to go," he admitted. "And now, because of me, we are hunted in two kingdoms. Perhaps you should go ahead on your own."

She laughed, though with little mirth. "Nomi at your service, Serenity."

"Karl," he said. "You *have* to remember I am Karl now."

"Then you will have to start talking like Karl the minstrel and not Aspen the prince," she told him.

"What do you mean?"

"Well, to start with, you sound like the toff you are, always saying things like 'I am not' when you should be saying 'I'm not,' and 'I am' when we underthings say 'I'm.'"

"But I *do not* talk like—"

"Don't." She laughed. Clearly she was laughing at him.

"Oh." He bit his lower lip. "I shall try."

"I'll try."

"You, too? Oh wait, I see." He managed a smile back at her. Then he said seriously, "I still do not know . . . er . . . don't know where we should be heading."

"Maybe we could stay with the trolls again," Snail said.

Aspen thought he saw a merry glint in her eyes.

"I . . . I'm sure the father would love to have us for dinner." He chuckled at his own retort, though he thought they both might be on the edge of hysteria.

"Neither one of us is fat enough for a meal," she pointed out.

He had to reluctantly agree she was right.

❖ ❖ ❖

THEY WALKED ON in silence for a bit, quickly leaving the cemetery and entering a wide field of barley where they scattered a family of partridge. The hen cackled at them with a great deal of anger before first flying toward Karl the minstrel's hat and then zigzagging away.

At the far end of the field, Aspen clambered over a low rock wall, then reached back for Snail's hand to help her over. He held on to her hand longer than he had to.

"There's a war coming," he said slowly, savoring the new way of talking.

"I know."

Her face was solemn. It was, he thought, a pleasant face, not beautiful like the twins, Sun and Moon. Not unreachable like theirs. But readable. Reliable. And loyal.

The woods had closed around them now, like a mother's arms, and that slowed their pace to a crawl. With it came a comforting darkness. Aspen knew it would make them safer even if, at the same time, it slowed them down.

"A war I started," he said it as if it were a confession, not to a human priest or to a dungeon master, with the hope of redemption or the ceasing of torture. Just said as one would to a friend.

He heard Snail snort and turned to look at her.

"You did no such thing!" she said derisively. "Remember what your mother told you."

"But I—"

"You were used by the drow, that Jack Daw. Manipulated. Almost killed!"

"That's true. But it was my responsibility—"

"*Your* responsibility?" she was almost shouting now. "You were a child! And where were your parents?"

"Shhhh!" he cautioned. They might be in the woods, but it was no guarantee they were alone.

In a softer voice she asked, "Well where *were* they?"

"Well, they were—"

"A thousand leagues away! And to your new family you were only a hostage, not a son, not a boy, but a piece in a game. A game of war. By Mab's heart, Serenity. I mean, Karl, I was raised an orphan, and I got more parenting from Mistress Softhands than you ever did from . . . from . . . anyone!"

"Maybe, but I—"

"No maybes, you—"

"Do not interrupt me again!" Aspen roared in exasperation.

"Now who's too loud?" Snail snapped, and then said quickly, "I'm sorry, Your Serenity." She didn't sound exactly sorry, though.

He shook his head. "No, Snail . . . er . . . Nomi. Not like that. I'm Karl, the minstrel, remember? And I just want a chance to speak."

"Go ahead then, Karl, speak as long as you need to."

He saw a small glow ahead, and guided them into a stand of wide-spaced birch and luminescent moss. The glow from the moss turned everything green-grey and black, as if the sun had been replaced by a witch moon while they'd talked.

He could see Snail's face clearly now, and tried to read her expression. *Angry? Hopeful? Expectant?* He had no idea.

Instead, he took a deep breath. "Everything you say is true. But I believe in . . ."

He stopped. *What do I believe in? What am I? Am I still a prince? Or am I truly Karl the minstrel now?*

"I believe in nobility," he finally said. Then, "Did you just snort again?"

"I did," Snail admitted. "I couldn't help it. My experiences with the nobility have been . . . less than, well, noble."

Aspen was about to argue for the nobility, but he stopped and forced himself to think. He thought about the nobles he knew: cruel Sun and Moon; manipulative Jack Daw; his father the king, who had sentenced him to death; King Obs, who would have adopted him as a son and killed him just as quickly.

"Mine, too, I suppose." He shook his head. "But I don't mean the nobles themselves, only what they are *supposed* to represent."

"And what's that?"

He thought about that for a moment. Tried to put it into words. "I believe in a nobility of purpose," he said.

"A nobility of purpose? What in all of Faerie does *that* mean? Sounds a lot like toff nonsense to me."

He scratched his chin. "I mean that I believe what my father says about the curse of rule. I believe in the responsibility of leaders to their people. And I believe I have . . . I've failed in that responsibility, not once, but twice now."

"Failed how?"

"Once when I let Jack Daw deceive me. And the second time when I let my mother free me."

"Bah!" She spat into the moss for emphasis.

"It's not what you believe, Nomi, it's what I believe. And I believe I have . . . um . . . I've failed as a hostage. I failed as a prince. I alone am responsible for this war."

And so saying what was lying heavy on his heart, he walked on, no longer able to look over at Snail, only looking down at his feet.

It took Aspen a few moments to realize Snail was not following him. Glancing back, he saw she was leaning against a birch tree, one hand idly picking at the bark.

"You haven't failed as a friend, Your Serenity." She looked up at him and smiled. "I mean Karl. The minstrel."

"Haven't I? Last I checked, we were alone in the woods with no home, no plan, and no allies. Oh, and no less than two armies gathering for war whose soldiers will have orders to kill us on sight!"

Snail stopped picking at the tree bark and stood up straight. She stepped toward Aspen and said, "And last time I checked, no less than two kings and one queen have ordered our deaths, and yet here we are, alive."

She stood in front of him now and grasped him by the arms. "*Alive!*" She looked hard into his eyes for a moment then backed away a step. "Listen, Karl. I'm sure you feel like you've lost everything."

"Well that is . . . that's comforting."

"I wasn't done. And now you're interrupting me."

"Sorry." He could not believe he just said that. *To an apprentice.* The world had turned upside down and he was not sure he was comfortable with that.

"You may have lost everything," she said, "but you don't see what you've gained." She walked a slow circle around the nearest tree, her hand on its trunk. "I didn't even see it till just now."

He watched her, confused. "See what?"

"It's been easier for me to understand, because I had nothing much to lose. Except my life."

"Understand what?"

"That we're free. We may not live to see next week. Mab's mercy! We might not live through this day and the night. But we're beholden to none. No one owns us. From here on, we make our own path."

"That *sounds* nice." And suddenly it did. *Wandering the world free of responsibility, free to come and go as one pleases, no king or kin sending one to stay in dirty, old fortresses full of dirty, mean creatures.* "But . . ."

"But?"

Aspen sighed. "But I am beholden."

"Princespeak."

"All right—*I'm* beholden. It means the same thing."

"And that is . . . ?"

"Listen, Snail—"

"Nomi," she corrected him.

"Right. Nomi. For you, freedom must be wonderful. You didn't choose your life—it was thrust upon you. No one—*especially* not me—would blame you for taking your new freedom and disappearing into the woods with it. But I want . . ." He paused. "No, I need—"

"A nobility of purpose," Snail finished for him.

He nodded and she stared at him with what he hoped was admiration but feared was pity. "Yes."

"And what is this purpose?" she asked.

"I don't know . . ." he began but stopped abruptly as he realized he *did* know. It was so obvious he wondered that it had taken him so long to think of it. *The fact that it's completely impossible and insane may have had something to do with it.* Quickly he shrugged the thought off. Folding his arms in front of him in what he hoped was a resolute pose, he said to Snail, "I'm going to stop the war."

He was very surprised that she didn't snort again. Instead, she asked him quite seriously, "And how are you going to do *that?*"

"I've absolutely no idea," he answered honestly. "But I know I'm going to need help."

She cocked her head at him, then looked away into the forest, as if mentally wandering its paths alone and seeing where they led. Then she sighed a bit theatrically and took two steps up to him and hooked her arm through his. "If I end up a kitchen slave again because of your 'nobility of purpose' I'm going to be very, *very* angry."

Chuckling, Aspen lead them out of the clearing's thin light and back into the dark of the thicker forest where they might be safe for the coming night.

"Good," he said. "I like you best when you're angry."

"And I," she countered, "like *you* best when you have a plan."

**END OF BOOK ONE OF THE SEELIE WARS TRILOGY**

## SNAIL AND PRINCE ASPEN'S STORY
## CONTINUES IN

Chased by two armies, Aspen and Snail find refuge with the actors of Professor Odds' traveling troupe—dodging soldiers, Border Lord berserkers, a hungry troll, a cloaked spy, and other assorted threats. Will they make it out? Is any place safe for the two of them? And who, exactly, is the mysterious Professor Odds, who seems to have his own hidden powers and agenda? Find out in the second book in the **Seelie Wars** trilogy!

# BE SURE TO CHECK OUT MORE
# NOVELS FROM JANE YOLEN!

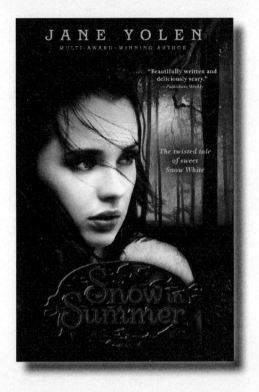

"Beautifully written and deliciously scary."

—*Publishers Weekly*

"Yolen spins an interesting variation of the classic Snow White story."           —*Kirkus Reviews*

"A well-imagined and well-told addition to the collections of retold fairy tales."           —*School Library Journal*

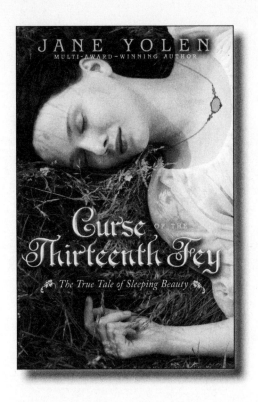

"Fans of more unconventional fantasy adaptations, such as Gregory Maguire's *Wicked*, will enjoy seeing an antagonist receive a rich compelling backstory."

—*School Library Journal*

"Inventive spin on Sleeping Beauty."     —*Publishers Weekly*

"Marvelous."     —*Booklist*

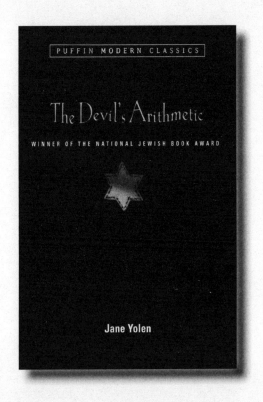

PUFFIN MODERN CLASSICS

The Devil's Arithmetic

WINNER OF THE NATIONAL JEWISH BOOK AWARD

Jane Yolen

★ "A triumphantly moving book."
—*Kirkus Reviews*, starred review

Winner of the
NATIONAL JEWISH BOOK AWARD and the
ASSOCIATION OF JEWISH LIBRARIES AWARD

**JANE YOLEN**, called "the Hans Christian Andersen of America" (*Newsweek*) and the "Aesop of the Twentieth Century" (*The New York Times*), is the author of well over three hundred books, including *Owl Moon, The Devil's Arithmetic,* and the How Do Dinosaurs . . . series. Her work ranges from rhymed picture books and baby board books through middle grade fiction, poetry collections, and nonfiction, and up to novels and story collections for young adults and adults. She has also written lyrics for folk-rock singers and groups, and several animated shorts. She's done voiceover work and talk radio. Her books and stories have won an assortment of awards—two Nebulas, a World Fantasy Award, a Caldecott Medal, the Golden Kite Award, three Mythopoeic Awards, two Christopher Medals, a nomination for the National Book Award, and the Jewish Book Award, among many others. She has been nominated three times for the Pushcart Prize. She is also the winner of the World Fantasy Association's Lifetime Achievement

Award, the Science Fiction Poetry Association's Grand Master Award, the Catholic Library's Regina Medal, the Kerlan Medal from the University of Minnesota, the 2012 de Grummond Medal, and the Smith College Alumnae Medal. Six colleges and universities have given her honorary doctorates.

Also worthy of note, she lost her fencing foil in Grand Central Station on a date and fell overboard while white-water rafting in the Colorado River, and her Skylark Award—given by NESFA, the New England Science Fiction Association— set her good coat on fire. If you need to know more about her, visit her website at www.janeyolen.com.

**ADAM STEMPLE** is an author, musician, web designer, maker of book trailers, and professional card player. He has published many short stories, and CDs and tapes of his music, as well as five fantasy novels—three for middle graders and two for adults. One of the middle grade novels, *Pay the Piper* (also written with Jane Yolen), won the 2006 *Locus* Award for Best Young Adult Book. The *Locus* plaque sits on the shelf next to two Minnesota Music Awards and trophies from his Fall Poker Classic and All In Series wins. His solo adult novel, *Singer of Souls*, was described by Anne McCaffrey as "one of the best first novels I have ever read."

For musings, music downloads, code snippets, and writing advice, visit him at adamstemple.com.